I Once  Walked

Barefoot

Among the snakes. Along a river. In its shallows
and silty sand.
Now, I walk a city park.

Mowed grass dotted with dog turds.
Admonishing placard strapped to
the sentinel redwood:

Please pick up after your pet.

Dodging snakes or dog shit,
which do you prefer?

Carol Teltschick

John's Motorcycle Storage and Rare Book Disposal,
Long Island New York

Cover Art by Tres Miller

Edited by Jan Wissmar

*This is a work of fiction. Names, characters, places,
brands, media, and incidents are either the product of the
author's imagination or are used fictitiously. Any
resemblance to similarly named places or to persons
living or deceased is unintentional.*

ISBN: 978-0-9979426-4-4

CONTENTS

DEDICATION

For my elders. Thank you.

PREFACE

I first met Carol in a drafty brick and mortar building in the heart of downtown Berkeley, a neighborhood whose better days were long gone but an area that still enchanted the eclectic with magic shops and coffee bars and of course, rare book stores. And so the occasional knife fight on the street was overlooked, and the homeless man, sleeping against the front door, was stepped over in the early morning by sleepy programmers clutching double lattes. My boss at the time kept crackers in the bottom drawer of his desk for the mice who came and went as they pleased. Any mention of an exterminator brought forth howls of indignation as did any attempt to enforce draconian measures as: no bikes allowed in the halls, no pornographic screen savers on your computers and no use of email for political diatribes.

It was Carol's job to wrangle technical information from a group of forty or so "code slingers," many of whom were unable to speak in anything but code. And she did it; on time and generally on budget. Something to do with her undeniably charming Texas drawl and promises of fruitcake. She often pulled programmers from the messy offices that defined their lives out into the sun for an afternoon game of soccer or a bike ride. But her dedication to clear, precise writing was always unwavering and, on points of grammar, she would never back down. Did I mention the many times I said "I never want to see that woman again!"

I love introductions that give you a sense of the writer as a human being so here we go. I think the Rolling Stones song "She's a Rainbow" describes Carol perfectly. She grows her own vegetables and eats them directly from the ground. I'm not even sure she washes them because a bit of dirt is probably good for your digestion. She likes to bathe each day in an antique clawfoot tub. Then, ever the environmentalist, she throws the bathwater out into the garden. If the city she lives in allowed it, she'd probably shoot the squirrel who dared to rob her of fresh peaches. And then make squirrel pie. In Kenya she was known as "Makena"—one who laughs. I'm sure they still remember her.

JT Twissel

COMMON OUTCOMES IN YOUNGER
WOMEN SUCH AS YOU

I have a tumor the size of Montana on my forehead but my doctor acts as though he can't see it.

"Let's do a CT scan," he says. "A CT scan with contrast dye. And an MRI."

I do the scans and the scans show nothing.

"Ok a PET scan," the doctor says. "Very effective."

"But why can't you just see it?" I ask.

"We use the tools we have," he says. "This is evidence-based medicine."

"But it's right here on my forehead. Can't you just...see it?"

"I can, but there's no way to prove it."

"What if you could prove it? What would you do then?"

"Well then I would offer you any number of things: Chemo, radiation, chemo-with-radiation. Surgery: to remove the tumor, some of your forehead and some of your brain. Drugs: for diarrhea, depression, nausea, to suppress hormones. Injections: to keep your bones from crumbling. Dietary supplements. Horse apples."

"Horse apples?"

"No, no...Sorry," the doctor says. "I just...see so many of you..."

He blinks in time with the fluorescent lighting.

"Well," I say, "will any of these things you're offering make me well?"

"No, of course not."

"I don't see why I should I do any of it then, if it won't make me well."

"Unfortunately, we don't yet have a cure for cancer," the doctor says. "This is the current standard of care."

I don't like the way he says *unfortunately*. Or *care*.

My forehead begins to throb, so I rub it a little, and am surprised to feel that the tumor has grown even bigger.

I can't think of anything to say or do after that, so I just sit there.

"Everybody gets the same treatments," the doctor says.

"But I don't want to do any of that," I repeat. "It sounds terrible."

"Well, I can't help you if you don't want to do the treatments or take the drugs."

I touch my forehead again. Is it really possible that the tumor has grown in the short time I've been sitting here in the doctor's office?

I give him a questioning look.

"Yes?" he says.

"Did it just get bigger?"

I'm sure he's going to say no, because tumors just don't grow that fast, but the doctor sighs and says,

"Unfortunately, this is a common outcome, especially in younger women such as you."

My heart sinks and I feel like I'm going to cry, which I don't want to do, at least not in front of this doctor. So I think, "fuck you," very strongly, and then I leave.

When I get outside the sun is shining and the trees are green and everything around me looks absolutely normal.

How can anything be normal when I have this gigantic tumor on my forehead? Or: How can I have this gigantic tumor on my head when everything else is absolutely normal?

I keep walking for a while and then I stop to stare at the trees. I see branches and trunks; shadows moving up and down; branches leading to smaller branches; branches even smaller; leaves that catch the light and shimmer, and also cast shadows. I think of bugs crawling on the trunk, in the branches, on the leaves, and I wonder if there's a way—any way at all—for me to make friends with this goddamned tumor.

THE NARCOLIZER

I was eleven years old when I first put horses to sleep. I didn't know how or why—didn't realize I was doing it. It was even a mystery to my big sister Devin, who is a natural when it comes to horses. Devin always rode with her shoulders back and her heels down, and was seldom corrected by our riding instructor. Whenever Devin was on a horse, she always had this look on her face that said: *What in the world could be better than this?*

Water, I would think. *Cool, clear water.*

I would squint my eyes against the dust and grit of the arena and imagine diving into the cool, clear lap pool at my parents' San Diego country club.

Then the riding instructor would tell me to sit up straight and look where I was going.

Devin never bragged about her riding skills, to me or anyone else. She just said that whenever she was with horses, things made sense to her. That horses were healthy and honest—the exact opposite of our parents' country club, which was sicko, and full of drunken liars.

Devin had just turned thirteen and as much as I envied her, I didn't like this new way she had of talking. It made me feel guilty about loving swimming instead of horses. And it made me think about my parents in a way that seemed wrong.

Whenever I dove into a pool, bad thoughts were instantly washed away, and I felt strong and clean and focused. I had never said this out loud but Devin knew. Devin always knew. "If swimming is what you really like, Jay-Jay, then *go* for it," she'd say. "Just remember that pool water isn't really clean, it's *chlorinated*."

The first time it happened was in late spring. School was not quite out, the weather was perfect, and Devin wanted to skip first period. "We'll leave early and ride all the way to the beach, Jay. You can swim in *real* water."

Devin had earned her apprenticeship status at the stables by being such a responsible rider. They gave her access to horses whenever she wanted.

I didn't want to ride all the way to the beach, or skip first period either. Devin wouldn't get in much trouble, she was starting high school the next year, but I was a 7th grader and first period was my favorite: biology. We were studying the history of vaccination.

But you couldn't argue with Devin. No point even trying.

We saddled our horses at 6:30 a.m. and led them to the trailhead. There was dew on the ground and the low swooping oaks on either side of the path were quiet. Devin had her current favorite, a big sorrel gelding named Trace, and I had Honey, a sweet-tempered golden mare.

At the mounting block, Devin reminded me to check Honey's girth. (I seldom got my girth right.) I turned and, without knowing why, put my hand on Honey's shoulder instead of the girth. Honey let out a long sigh, dropped her head and lay down on her side. She stretched out completely flat along the ground, with her neck and legs fully extended. Her nose was tipped up and her wavy golden tail fanned out behind her.

It scared me so badly it felt like my brain went numb.

Honey groaned and closed her eyes.

"What the hell," Devin said. "Get her up."

I didn't know how.

Devin led Trace over, handed me his reins and knelt down next to Honey. She stroked and clicked and clucked and nudged. She talked soft and she talked hard. But Honey wouldn't budge.

Trace tossed his head and snorted. I was slightly afraid of Trace but stood my ground. "Quiet," I said, in the roughest voice I could muster.

I turned back to Devin and asked, "What's wrong with her?"

"She might be foundering," Devin said. "Or colicking."

Devin had heard about things that could make a horse sick but didn't know what to do next. She said she was going to have to call our instructor, who would probably call a vet. We would get in trouble but it would save Honey.

Trace tossed his head again but by then I was so worried about Honey I forgot to be afraid of him. I put a hand on his shoulder and said, "Shh. Calm down."

He let out a low groan and lay down, stretching out along the ground just like Honey.

Devin shot me a look that was half fear and half murder. Then she pulled out her cell phone.

After that, our relationship shifted. Devin rode and I swam. In the fall, Devin went to an expensive preppie high school and became known as a rebel, fighting all things dishonest and unnatural. I stayed on at the middle school, joined the Science Club and was elected president. Everyone but Devin started calling me by my full name Jaylee instead of Jay-Jay.

At home Devin and I still talked, but not about anything that mattered.

We especially did not talk about Trace and Honey. According to our instructor, the horses had bamboozled us. They had both clambered to their feet, as normal as anything, the instant the instructor had arrived. But I could tell by Devin's face that she did not think we'd been bamboozled.

The mystery filled the widening space between us.

In the summer before Devin became a senior and I became a sophomore, our parents took us to Aspen on a vacation. Devin declined, claiming that all of our family vacations were elitist bullshit but they wouldn't let her stay home.

I didn't say a word. I thought I was staying neutral.

After tennis camp and before river rafting, our parents told us they'd scheduled us on a group trail ride to the base of the Maroons, a mountain range known for its dark red slopes and frosty white peaks.

When I wondered if our parents were doing this as a concession to Devin, she (still able to read my thoughts) said it was just another "must do" recommended by their country club friends.

The ranch was a topnotch operation and the horses looked so good Devin dropped her sulky attitude the moment she saw them. A ranch hand brought us a pair of matching bays and all of a sudden, I began to think it was going to be a fun ride. This was a foolish idea since I was the one who was about to ruin things.

It went almost exactly like the last time—except with witnesses. We soon had two horses lying on the trail. The ranch hand said it was the damnedest thing he'd ever seen.

I never asked my parents why they scheduled that ride, or why things kept going so bad between them and Devin. I didn't want to know. I was on a roll. I was getting straight A's at school. I was on the swimming team and had a lot of friends who thought I was cool.

While I kept doing things that everyone praised me for, Devin kept doing things that made people shake their heads and mutter, "What's she trying to prove?"

She got drunk and fell in the pool to show them how stupid they were. When she was nineteen, she dropped out of college and got a job at the Dairy Queen to show solidarity with the working classes.

My parents, and everyone at the country club, called her an unappreciative little smartass.

Devin didn't care. "They think if they run me down enough I'll stop, but that's not how it works."

It drove me crazy that she never, even for an instant,

seemed to doubt herself. Did she really care about the working classes or was she just trying to piss our parents off?

When Devin was twenty, she moved away without telling anyone. I learned through a friend's older brother that she was in San Francisco. It was 1967, the summer of love.

"Figures," was all my parents said.

She came home for Christmas that December and it was a Passion Play. Everyone thought they were the Savior but acted like Pontius Pilate. Except me, of course, I still thought I was being neutral. I had just completed my first year of pre-med study and was busy developing the foundation of hubris upon which careers in Western medicine are built.

The years went by, and no one heard from Devin. We didn't forget her. We just sort of *erased* her. She became a myth. I envied her, loved her, disapproved of her, and wanted to cut ties with her, all at the same time.

I became a surgeon, and after only two years in a private hospital, went to work for Kaiser Permanente. I was proud of myself for working at Kaiser instead of building a lucrative private practice. I believed in preventive check-ups, didn't cringe at the term *holistic* and thought of myself as a progressive who would gradually, and carefully, improve the medical system from within.

I started out in gastrointestinal and before long, at least half of my cases were related to cancer. In the 80's, the rates of breast cancer shot so high, I was encouraged by my director to change specialties. Most surgeons were still men back then, and the director thought that women with breast cancer would appreciate the greater sensitivity of a woman. So I set out to help and was certain that I could. My hubris grew to a new level.

Over a thousand mastectomies later, while doing a post-op exam, I told one of my patients that her scars looked beautiful and she hauled off and kicked me square in the gut.

I went down like a horse, and lay there awhile, thinking. I remembered Honey and the beautiful bay horses in Aspen. I wondered what Devin would do and for the first time in years, I heard her voice in my head. "Well in the first place," she said. "I'd never cut off a woman's breasts to help her. Are you crazy? Start with an apology."

I got to my feet and apologized to the woman. She grabbed her clothes and burst into angry tears. I cried too. Sensitive surgeon becomes even better at her job. The next thousand mastectomies went a lot better. For me.

When I was fifty-four, I had a dream. Things were reversed. I was the one who was sick and Devin was the one telling me how to get well. "Look inside your beautiful self," she said. "Do you really think this is the appropriate kind of cancer for you?"

I woke in a sweat. What did she mean? That I had chosen the wrong career path, or that I was about to be diagnosed with breast cancer myself? I began to cry and tremble with fear, knowing that I could never subject myself to mastectomy or chemo.

The next day, while I was still sick with fear and still trying to interpret the dream, Devin called. Her voice was raw but it sounded like her. She was in a mental hospital in Seattle, dying of liver failure.

"They think I'm fucking crazy," she said, and laughed.

In a sweep of something that felt like a mega-hot flash, I realized why I had "learned" to put horses to sleep.

"Devin," I said softly, "if you want some help at the end, I'm here for you." Sensitive surgeon helps derelict sister die with dignity.

"Oh, you goddamned doctors," Devin said with a snort that turned into a coughing fit. "You do the vilest things and call it helping."

That was my big sister. None of us ever managed to fool her.

JEANNIE, JEANNIE AND BLISS

"Beauty is a simple passion,
but oh my friends, in the end
you will dance the fire dance in iron shoes."

— *Anne Sexton*

Jeannie opened her eyes and saw white. White walls, white sheets, white light. She felt buoyant, and airy. Had she already had the surgery? She reached down to feel her thighs. They were as massive as ever, and it hurt to move any little part of her big fat body. She groaned.

"So you're not dead then?"

The voice came from a bed on the other side of the room. Jeannie looked over and saw an expanse of sheets, only slightly stained with the presence of a small, wizened woman of indeterminate age. Her head was bony and crowned with a frizzy aurora of mouse-brown hair, giving the appearance of a dead flower ready to drop from the stalk of her neck. An IV hung from a contraption over her bed, dripping fluid into the left arm. The eyes were burned out cinders, but still hot enough to scorch with a sidewise glance.

"Is this a hospital?" Jeannie asked.

"I don't know," the creature said, "I don't know

anything except that you've been snoring like a fat cow the whole afternoon."

Ok, Jeannie thought, I'm in a hospital—or an asylum. She began to search for a buzzer, or some way to call a nurse.

She found the buzzer and a nurse in perky pink materialized in the doorway, leaning her bouffant hairdo into the room then following it inside. "Jeannie," she said, nodding at Jeannie, "and Jeannie," nodding at the creature. "Have you introduced yourselves?"

"Not exactly," Jeannie said.

The creature made a gurgling noise and turned her face to the wall.

The nurse checked their charts for last names. "Ah yes," she said aloud, "Jeannie Stanton and Jeannie Bright." She tilted her head to one side and swept the room with a pretty smile. "Miss Stanton..." she said, turning her smile on Fat Jeannie. "Are we feeling any better?"

God help me, Jeannie thought, it's an insane asylum.

"Please," she said to the nurse. "Can you remind me why I'm here?"

"You had a bicycle accident. Mild concussion. Bruised kidney."

"Oh," Jeannie said, disappointed. She was hoping that she'd finally found a way to afford her weight loss surgery and was experiencing mild post-surgical amnesia.

"Ok then. Just tell me three things: when will a doctor be coming to see me, when can I be moved to another room, and when do you serve lunch?"

"Your doctor will be by later this afternoon, there are no other rooms available, and you just missed lunch. You slept right through it, honey."

The nurse left, and the creature said, "Of course, the first thing they always want to do is eat."

"That's right," Jeannie answered. "And everyone hates the fat lady, even horrible little dried-up creatures."

"*Especially* horrible little dried-up creatures," the creature hissed.

☙

Fat Jeannie was on the phone, talking to her sister. "You mean you actually rode your bike right into the side of a Domino's Pizza van?" her sister said. "Does this mean you're not coming to my wedding?"

"I don't know," Jeannie said. "I guess it would be a perfect excuse…"

"Excuse? Don't you want to come?"

"I did. I really did. But now I think it might be more fun to lie around in the hospital eating Jell-O than fly to Boston to march down the aisle as a green taffeta monstrosity."

"Jeannie! I can't believe you are so…mixed up. Everyone else thinks the dresses are perfect."

Jeannie sighed into the phone. Only another fat woman would understand what it's like to stand before your mirror and think: three inches, all over. To hate the sight of yourself so much that the most enjoyable thing you can imagine is a sharp blade, slicing through the fat, sending it far, far away, forever, and who cares if the blade is really that sharp?

"They're bringing lunch, I have to go," Jeannie said and hung up.

The wedding was in April, only two weeks away, and liposuction, or some form of surgical removal, was the only means by which Karen could get thin enough in time to be bridesmaid. Leave it to her sister to insist on shiny green taffeta. Her sister who was beautiful and slim, and marrying a handsome young doctor just as her mother had always dreamed she would.

Jeannie, of course, was the *other* daughter. The loser daughter, whose life had been an endless succession of futile diets. The chocolate diet, the water diet, the meat diet, the fruit diet, the don't-eat-anything-after-6 a.m. diet, the grapefruit with powdered elk horn diet…to name just a few. She had done the sit-ups and gone for the hikes. She had answered the ads in parking lots and on street corners: *Lose 10 lbs a day! Call now!* She had once, regrettably, gone for a hike while on the chocolate diet, which works by giving you diarrhea.

Standing in line at the grocery store, while her hands were busy unloading her basket of non-fat, low-carb, sugar-free, reduced-salt items, her brain battled the display of women's magazines. It was a love-hate kind of thing, as contradictory as the glossy covers of the magazines themselves, where the taut bodies of barely-dressed models (*Discover the Secret of Dressing Sexy*) sprouted from the pruriently portrayed curves and surfaces of luscious cakes and come-hither pies (*Eat your Favorite Desserts and Still Lose Weight. It's easy!*).

Yet even in the midst of all her worshiping-detesting-denying-binging, despite her unflagging contributions to the fifty billion dollars spent every year on dieting and beauty products in North America alone, Jeannie sometimes ventured into rebel territory. For example, instead of buying a new pair of sweatpants and joining a gym, she sold her car and bought a mud-spattered mountain bike. Without even bothering to stock her closet with a brand-new set of "slim Jeannie" clothes, she jumped on the bike and went. Every day, everywhere, rain or shine, she pedaled. Red hair frizzed and flying in the wind, flesh bulging from the confines of her full-support sport bra and stretchy latex cycling shorts. Faster and faster still, until her heart was wild and furious and she was sure that this, this extreme offering, would finally be the one to do the trick. The pounds would melt away and her searching and her suffering would end. It had to.

At dinnertime, the nurse waltzed in with tubes dangling from one hand and a tray balanced on the other. Jeannie eased herself into a sitting position. She was so sore she could hardly wiggle a toe, but her appetite blazed like a house afire. The nurse deposited the tray on the wheeled table next to Jeannie's bed then continued toward the creature's side of the room.

Jeannie pulled the tray close and examined its contents. A cube of red Jell-O quivered weakly, and a sloppy looking entrée of diced chicken and noodles oozed against a mound of uniformly cut green beans. Across the room, the nurse was hanging a bag onto the framework of the creature's IV contraption and adjusting the tubes.

Apparently one tube carried nourishment into the emaciated body, and another carried waste out and away.

"Bon *appétit*," Jeannie said and stabbed a forkful of noodles.

Still fiddling with the creature's tubes, the nurse told Jeannie to expect a follow-up MRI and urine analysis the next morning.

When the nurse was gone and Jeannie had savored the final wiggly mouthful of her strawberry Jell-O, the room grew heavy with an atmosphere of unwelcome satiation. Checking the ceiling for any new cracks that might have occurred since lunch, Jeannie decided to venture a bit of conversation. "If I stay here long enough, will I get as skinny as you?"

There was a swishing sound then the creature emitted a rusty laugh. "That might take a while."

"How long has it been since you've eaten solid food?"

Again, the laugh. "How long have you been fat?"

Jeannie sighed. "Oh, I don't know...Since I was twelve, thirteen? My entire life?"

"One forgets," said the creature.

Yes, Jeannie thought, one forgets, and felt her bones grow weary, as though they might disintegrate, melt into her fat and stop holding her up. She closed her eyes and saw a five-year old girl, pretty in a powder blue dress with puffy sleeves, white sash tied in a perfect bow at her back. Hair of red-gold, silky to the touch but Lord Have Mercy, how to make it hold a curl. It is impossible, so terribly impossible, and the girl's mother is desperate. Bobby pins, curling irons, permanents, cries of anguish. No one knows how hard it was to create this pretty girl, but see the result and be satisfied. No one cares how pretty girls are made, the important thing is that we have them.

Was it true that the pretty little girl had grown into a fat abomination, crashing around on a mud-spattered mountain bike? Perhaps she was some other Jeannie, a lithe and agile tomboy, racing, tumbling, laughing, King-of-the-Mountain Jeannie, hating the powder blue dress, the puffy sleeves, the golden curls and the stiff, patent leather shoes. She could not move, or breathe or run. They would not let her out. Yes, it probably was another Jeannie, a girl who ran so swiftly that she turned into a tangle of plastic tubes. After so many years and so many lost battles, one does tend to forget. And who would want it otherwise?

Fat Jeannie's mother was on the phone. "Jeannie, honey…how are you? I've been so worried…"

"I'm ok, Mother. Sore, but ok."

"Well what were you doing on that bike? Riding through heavy traffic the way you do, it's just…"

"I like riding my bike."

"…a bit extreme."

"My fat is extreme, so I am extreme."

"Now don't start talking nonsense. Your doctor says that you'll be up and around in less than a week. You can still make the wedding. We'd love to see you."

"So come visit me. They're keeping me one more day to watch my kidney." She pictured her kidney lying on a bed of fat, male doctors gathered around it, gazing down in silent disgust.

"Oh, honey, I wish I could. But it's such a long flight to Oakland and we're so busy here…And anyway, you'll soon be here for the wedding, won't you?"

"To tell you the truth, I'm having trouble with the green taffeta."

"Jeannie! Green is lovely with red hair."

"So they say. But hey, lunch is here, so I have to go. I didn't get a chance to tell you about the strawberry Jell-O, but I'll fill you in next time."

Jeannie plonked down the phone. When the devoted mother is busy helping the fairy princess daughter prepare for her nuptial celebrations she has no time for the fat clumsy sister. But as her mother always said: "Don't be jealous. It's impolite, and makes awful lines around the mouth."

A rustling sound came from the other side of the room, all dead leaves and dry sticks, then a whisper: In China, it is the mother who binds the daughter's feet.

Was the creature reading her mind, or had she muttered something aloud? Jeannie was just about to ask when the bouffant-haired nurse waltzed in and handed her a tray. The Jell-O was green instead of red.

After consuming everything on her tray, including the green Jell-O, which was utterly despicable, Jeannie glanced across the room at the creature, the other Jeannie, whose head barely dented her big fluffy pillow, whose body formed the merest bulge beneath her sheets. Who knows… it might be nice to become a creature. To simply lie down at long last in a clean white bed and do nothing whatsoever except grow smaller and smaller with every single breath you take.

"I know a woman who had her mouth wired shut to lose weight," Jeannie said.

The creature stirred, and hacked out a bitter laugh. "I know someone who consulted an astrologer."

"I know someone who had herself hypnotized," Jeannie answered.

"I know someone who took diet pills and had a heart attack," the creature said.

"Someone who got gangrene from liposuction and had her leg amputated," Jeannie said.

"…someone who had part of her stomach removed."

"Some women get staples instead of removal."

"Yes. The woman I know removed."

"Was it you?"

"Hell no."

She is not stupid, this Jeannie Stanton, this Jeannie Bright, but sometimes her brain does not work right. She is tired, like a mule toiling after a carrot that dangles before her nose, trying not to notice that the carrot has been fastened to a stick that is attached to her own back. She plods on and the world spins past without a sound. People seeking wealth, people seeking friends, fame, power; a cure for cancer, cheaper laundry detergent and international peace. People working, climbing mountains, taking showers, looking for their keys. Some of them are listening to a lovely song.

The Jeannies toil on, hearing nothing but their own bodies crying for transformation.

(◊)

On Jeannie Stanton's last day in the hospital, shortly after lunch, the creature said, "I've been wondering, if you ever saw me in the news."

"You in the news? What for?"

"My art. Sculptures about beauty, and fashion."

"Sure, and I'm the Duchess of Windsor," Jeannie snorted.

"Believe it or not, it's true."

"Tell me about it then." Might as well listen, what else was there to do?

And so the creature began her story: "I was standing in front of the full-length mirror in my bedroom, trying to stuff myself into a pair of jeans that were too tight and all of a sudden I got this flash memory of me and my high school girlfriends throwing ourselves onto a bed and using coat hangers to zip our jeans. And there I was, thirty-seven years old, still fighting the same old battle. Still promising myself I would lose five pounds by the end of the week. I wanted to tear off the jeans and cut them to ribbons. But instead, I merely looked at myself in the mirror. Really looked."

Jeannie sighed and muttered, "This is not going to end well..."

"I was not obese," the creature continued, ignoring Jeannie's comment, her voice gaining surprising force. "I was just, as they say, a little chunky. This was phrase I detested because it described me so perfectly. At five foot two and 135 pounds, I was indeed a chunky little burro. 'Is this how you would treat a burro?' I said aloud, which made me laugh, and I wondered what would happen if I decided to just cut the crap and stop trying to look like women on billboards and magazine covers."

"Burros are cute," Jeannie said. "If you're a burro."

"I decided to purge my life instead of my body," the creature said. "Appetite regulators, energy boosters, mood adjusters. My bathroom scale, which I consulted at least twice a day. Clothes that pinched or squeezed in private places; restricted movement; anything that wasn't comfortable." She could have built a mountain there was so much crap. And she was throwing it all out. Forever.

Jeannie Stanton thought of her own closet, full of clothes that didn't fit. Clothes that made her promise herself to lose weight fast. Clothes that made her feel guilty for being fat, for being a bad shopper, for having a messy closet, for taking up more space in the world than she should. She thought of the blow dryer in her bathroom with its five attachments and fifteen settings. Her curling iron, which looked like an instrument of torture. Which was an instrument of torture. Five bottles of conditioner to repair damage caused by the curling iron. Hair clips, hair ties, hairpins, hair bands. So many items of control.

The creature droned on, naming more things she had thrown away: eye shadow, eye liner, eyebrow pencil, eye cream, mascara, eyelash curlers, night cream, day cream, wrinkle cream; lipstick, lip contour, lip gloss, foundation, translucent powder, blusher, blemish repair, nail polish, nail polish remover, makeup remover. "I worked all day and into the night," she said. "Piling and heaping it up, stuffing it into trash bags, and when I was finally done, I was struck by the sheer wastefulness of it all. Instead of hauling the clothes down to Goodwill and throwing the rest away, I wondered if could make something. Maybe have a little fun."

"Oh, you mean, like, art?" Jeannie said. She didn't want to be sarcastic, but the story was becoming irksome, a sort of reverse self-admiring.

"Yes, like art," the creature hissed. "I scrounged some wire and a roll of twine and got to work." Twisting, rolling, weaving, wrapping, gluing things together, the minutes flowed into hours. The materials came to life in her hands. And when she finally pulled back and looked, she saw that she had created a trilogy of forms: Style Scarecrows.

They weren't half bad but she knew she could do better.

Over the following months, floating through the exigencies of regular life with the bare minimum of attention, she completed a course in welding, then began visiting the local recycling center. When she put the finishing touches on her first success, she knew she'd done it. Rising up from a fifty-five pound base made from false eyelashes set in clear epoxy, was a shimmering tower of eyelash curlers, spot-welded together. She named it Eyes

Open and put it in her front yard next to a blooming fuchsia.

Satisfaction with the outcome of Eyes Open emboldened her, yet she had to admit, she sometimes caught herself worrying about how she looked in her practical, comfortable clothes and no makeup. She was dumpy. Letting herself go. Depressed. Becoming a lesbian? Yet at the same time: a rising sense of buoyancy, a single-minded contentedness.

She took down all her mirrors and used them in her next creation. Its base was triangular, and molded from the flesh-gouging jeans and thongs that had once chafed and blistered the tender cleft between her buttocks. Atop the triangular base were the five mirrors on metal arms, forming a vortex that endlessly reflected a colorful heap of cosmetics, foam rollers, and curling irons. She titled it: Woman, Thy Name is Vanity, then crossed out the word Vanity and replaced it with Marketing.

In her front yard, next to Eyes Open, the effect of Thy Name was stunning. Energy seemed to spark and flow between the two sculptures and, standing before them, she felt sure she had embarked upon a journey that would lead to something big.

Jeannie Stanton found herself liking the artistic concepts and wanted to comment, but did not dare interrupt. The creature was obsessed with her telling, reliving it all.

"Over the course of the next year, I filled my yard with art," the creature said. "I made a twenty-foot-tall Hair Village from wigs and hair extensions. I made Helping Hands from fake fingernails. A diorama called Ready Reversibles from products used to straighten hair and curl hair, juxtaposed with products for tanning and bleaching the skin. A Tummy Toner Tower, made of exercise videos.

"News of my yard-art spread, and people began stopping by to look and ponder and chat. Five of these people were men who asked me out. One was a medical intern who donated breast implants that had ruptured and leaked toxic fluid into unsuspecting chest walls. From these I made my award-winning Sili Con.

"I got a grant, and quit my day job. I turned my garage into a studio. I started a website and women from all over the world began sending me their stories and discarded beauty products."

Could any of this be true, Jeannie Stanton wondered. Could it?

The creature kept going: It was her 39th birthday, and she felt like celebrating. She bought a double dark chocolate cake from the esteemed Rubicon Bakery and called her new best friends, Sally and Tim, a middle-aged couple, who were also artists. Sally and Tim brought wine and they spent the afternoon hopping from studio to studio, visiting other artists they knew. It couldn't have been more perfect. She had finally learned to enjoy life.

Indeed, this new way of doing things might well have carried her happily and comfortably forward into old age, if it hadn't been for the Bra Ball.

The Bra Ball was not a project she had set her heart on, but when her plan for something based on Botox needles and Halloween masks didn't work out, she regretfully turned to the more dangerous medium of women's undergarments.

At first she thought to work exclusively with Wonder Bras but then decided to welcome the entire gamut: worn out bras, discarded bras, bras that lifted, bras that flattened, bras that concealed and bras that exposed. She posted a "call for bras" on her website and her studio was soon clogged with them. She wound them together as one would wind bits of string, and kept going until her bra-ball weighed upwards of 400 pounds and stood nearly eighteen feet high.

Word of her Bra Ball spread, and as she was trying to figure out a plan for moving it to her front yard, a reporter from the San Francisco Chronicle called and requested an interview. He came the next day and, with a click that Jeannie Bright barely heard, snapped the photograph that would change her life.

It appeared in the Sunday Lifestyle section: Jeannie Bright high on a ladder next to her Bra Ball with a lacy, black bra dangling from her hand. Sexy Berkeley Lady Expresses Herself with Bras. She couldn't believe her eyes. The woman standing on the ladder—a woman with no makeup and wearing the same old pair of loose-fitting dungarees and faded blue t-shirt that she always wore— had never looked better. Is that really me, she wondered, this woman who exuded such a confident, athletic air, this woman with a smile so open and attractive? That night, as she soaped herself in the shower and watched the water run over her, she was tempted to go out and buy a mirror.

The next day, she was visited by a reporter from Channel 5 TV and appeared on the evening news for fifteen seconds. The day after that, her Bra Ball picture ran in the Oakland Tribune and the Berkeley Daily Planet. People were intrigued by this lady doing weird things with bras. But no one except the Daily Planet asked about her other art pieces. They just wanted bras. It pissed her off, and she decided to write letters of protest to the editors and station managers.

Halfway through the first letter, she got the call. A professional, detached-sounding voice glided through the wire, slipping from one world into another, right into Jeannie Bright's ear. "This is Trish," the voice said, "calling on behalf of Playboy magazine. We saw your story and wonder if you'd be interested in doing a spread."

A spread?

"Ms. Bright?" Trish said. "Hello?"

A sound emerged from Jeannie's mouth and Trish said, "We envision you in a new wave, industrial-type setting, very hip, maybe holding a blow torch or something."

"Would I be nude...or what?"

"Yes, nude, of course."

Jeannie put her lips closer to the mouthpiece. "I might not look good nude."

"Oh you will," Trish said. "You will. Our photographers are the best."

Jeannie fished a scrap of paper from a drawer full of aluminum foil pieces and twisty-ties and scribbled down Trish's number. "Sure, no problem, I'll let you know by next week..."

She hung up and lay down on the floor. She closed her eyes.

Linoleum pressed into her back, cool, like a drink of water.

Water...nice...

The back of her head, her shoulders, buttocks, her heels fused with the linoleum, flowed into it, and brought peace.

Ten years ago, an offer to appear in Playboy might very well have touched her like the wand of the fairest fairy godmother. But now. Now, she was a savvy thirty-nine year-old, an accomplished artist, and she didn't give a shit about looking good for Playboy.

Right?

Right?

She called Sally and Tom. "What?" Sally said. "I can't believe you're even considering this. You sound like a reformed druggie who has just been offered a free delivery of cocaine and heroin."

But Tom said, "Go for it, baby! Exploit the exploiters!"

Sally was angry. "Tom! I can't believe you're saying this!"

Jeannie phoned other friends, and more friends, and found that opinions were fairly equally divided between no way and why not.

No need to decide in a rush, Jeannie told herself. Wait a few days. Sleep on it.

But the sleep was not good, and the days were not peaceful. She dawdled around the house, wandering from room to room, unable to work, inaction breeding indecision, indecision begetting inaction. She ate poorly and, lacking the motivation to cook or even make a sandwich, drove to the 24-hour Safeway. Came home with chips and sour cream, and two big slabs of lemon cake that reminded her of tombstones.

Later, bloated and belching, she crawled into bed and decided she would not call Trish, or anyone, ever.

Days became weeks, weeks became months, and everyday she squandered her time, stuffing herself with junk, hating what was happening to her, hating herself more with every bite.

She gained twenty pounds. Started a fast. Broke the fast. Found that fasting was the only way to stop the eating. It was eat or starve, nothing in between. Eating was animalistic and ugly. Starving allowed her to float, disconnected, above everything, like an angel.

From there the fall was swift and welcome.

Once in the hospital, at ninety-two pounds, the tubes took care of everything. No decisions, no feelings, no self. She was levitating, disappearing, and it had all felt just fine. Until Fat Jeannie showed up.

Fat Jeannie sat bolt upright and stared at the creature. Thirty-nine? Forty? She looked more like seventy. But the story had caused Fat Jeannie's heart to lift and fall by turns, to twist with sympathy, soar with admiration, and recoil in disbelief.

In the end, disbelief won out. The creature was sick and shriveled and out of her mind, dreaming up stories to redeem her pathetic life.

Subsequent conversations between the two Jeannies were brief and awkward, and the next morning, when Fat Jeannie was released from the hospital, they barely mumbled goodbye.

Leaving the hospital, Jeannie Stanton stepped lightly into her old world, feeling she had been away for months instead of three days. All the familiar scenes seemed slightly distorted, as though someone had drawn sharp lines along all of its edges. When she tried to blink the lines away, an airy feeling expanded in her head.

That night, bedding down, she closed her eyes and purposefully emptied her mind of everything. No wedding, no creature, no decisions. All she needed was rest. Yet the moment sleep descended, she began to dream that she was at her sister's wedding. Walking up the aisle. Stark naked. Fat. Carrying an armless, faceless mannequin zipped neatly into the green taffeta dress.

While Jeannie Stanton dreamed, the creature continued to wizen in her white hospital bed. Flesh to skin, skin to bones, bones to dust. Reducing herself to a heap of ash and a single repetitive thought: do not eat, do not eat, do not eat.

The thought shot through space, pierced Jeannie Stanton's sleeping hindbrain and planted itself there.

NO BEAUCOUP BISOUS

Ten American Women Traveling in Africa

"We Africans are very amorous," Ousmane told Teresa with an adoring look, "but don't let it cause you any problems."

It seemed true. The Senegalese men seemed completely ready for romance, and they were beginning to see that we California women were not. We had worked too hard, training ourselves to be independent and cautious. And in California, the men are independent and cautious too. They don't crowd around us with such full-on amorous intensity, charmed by our smallest gesture or facial expression.

In Senegal, we are neither trained nor independent. We cannot speak for ourselves, cook for ourselves, or even walk down the street by ourselves. But no problem, because all the young men who want to fall in love in with us are constantly at our sides, ready and willing to help. Yes, we are cautious but we are also needy, and curious, so it is not long before we have an entourage of boyfriends, following us everywhere.

Why do They Like Us So Much? We Need to Figure It Out

"They like us because we have everything and they have nothing."

"No, it's the same as anywhere. They just want *coochie*, like all men everywhere. That's all they really care about."

"They want green-cards, don't they? They want to come to America because they think America is some of kind of paradise."

"Yeah, a paradise full of beautiful blonds and high-paying jobs."

"Don't start with the color thing. They seem to like brunettes as well as blonds."

"They seem to like blacks as well as whites."

"They just like Americans."

"They just like women!"

A Conversation With Babou, our Senegalese Trip Leader

Babou thinks that we would have to know as much about life in Senegal as he does before we could really understand what these guys want. It's too complicated for him to explain, so instead he issues another of his warnings. "Watch out," he says, "these guys are going to lie to you. Especially the young ones. They lie because they think they have to. They don't believe you will like them if they tell the truth."

"Sounds like men everywhere," Kelly says.

"Believe me or not," Babou says. "I can tell you what they are doing and even what they are thinking because when I was young I was exactly like them. They all have Senegalese girlfriends here, and plenty of them, but they're telling you that they don't, aren't they? Isn't that what they are telling you?"

"Ousmane said I'm his first," Teresa says and starts laughing. "I'm waiting for the right *woooman*," she says, imitating Ousmane's voice and what she calls his "dork expression" perfectly.

"Boubacar said he hasn't had sex in five years!"

"H-a-a-e-e-e-e!" Babou thinks this is hilarious. "Believe

me or not, those boys are having sex."

"And Omar said he doesn't like having Senegalese girlfriends because they make him bring them presents and pay for everything and he can't do that because he doesn't have any money."

"Yeah, they'd rather go out with us so we can pay for everything!"

"Look," Babou says. "Do you know how many girlfriends I had when I lived here?"

We look at him expectantly.

"One hundred."

"Babou!" we scream. "That's too many!"

"It is," he says. "But I had them. Believe me or not. I'm a musician, and when I lived here, I was traveling everywhere. E-e-v-e-e-r-y-y-where, in Senegal, Gambia, Guinea Bissau. I performed everywhere. And everywhere I stopped, I had a different girlfriend."

"And you told all of them they were your only girlfriend?"

"Of course!"

"Why?"

"Because they wouldn't like to hear otherwise."

"Women are disgusting!" Kelly says. "As soon as they see a man on stage, they just want to fuck him!"

"That's right," Teresa says. "And it's the same at home. We're not any different, are we?"

"Well," Willa says diplomatically, "it could be a case of loving the artist and not the man."

"But these guys hanging around us aren't musicians. Or anything. Most of them don't even have jobs. There're just regular normal young men, living a normal life with their normal families."

"I think they're nice guys. Regular, normal, nice guys.

They seem sincerely sweet and why should we be mad at them for wanting to get to know us?"

"There are just too many of them."

"They lie to us."

"Tell them *no beaucoup bisous!*"

"What does that mean?"

"No lots of kisses."

"But they're fun to be with. They're good dancers."

"They're fun and they're funny. They can hardly even talk to us, but they still know how to make us laugh."

"You can really relax and be yourself. They take you just how you are."

"That's because they're relaxed themselves. They are just so...so...relaxed. So *human!*"

"They're just themselves."

"They have good manners. They always treat us nice."

"Too much nice is not nice. It's a pain in the butt to be adored twenty-four hours a day."

"It's all fake anyway. Listen to what Babou is trying to tell us."

"Babou, are you trying to say they don't even really like us?"

"Like you? Of course they like you!" Babou shouts.

And then he laughs uproariously.

CHEATERS

"A woman is a common maize cob for every man
with teeth to bite." This means that every woman
is beautiful and every man is willing to
communicate with her.

—School girl's interpretation of a Kenyan proverb

Mama Njoki

Tomorrow I will take some bananas to the American. I
will give her the bananas and I will try to find out about
the money.

They say that she was sent here by Priscilla's husband,
Henry, who left Meru Town five long years ago. Gone to
live in America, and what he is doing there even his own
wife does not know.

Eh! Make no speculation about the boy at Priscilla's
breast. Henry has been back to visit twice in five years
time. You have only to look once at the boy to be sure that
he is Henry's. See the round expanse of forehead? How the
face narrows dramatically beneath the cheek bones,
pinching the mouth in so and causing the teeth to protrude
severely for want of space in the jaw? Ah, no, Henry is not
a handsome man, nor is he known for his kindness.

His property, however, is no cause for shame. Four
hectares of good shamba which produces enough cabbages,

bananas, carrots, potatoes and what-have-you for his family to eat. A stone house of five rooms, two cows, and a yard full of chickens. Another small house for his mother, and behind that, two separate latrines with two separate doors and raised concrete floors. And in the main house, a telephone, just so Henry can call his wife from America but *eh!* he never does.

That is Henry's place, there, near the end of this red dirt road.

Priscilla

Starting down the red dirt road that leads to her home, Priscilla walks slowly, perspiring steadily beneath a long-sleeved dress of polyester knit. The European fabric and cut of the dress contrast falsely with the rich reds and vibrant greens of the maize fields that surround her.

"Makena," she mutters.

The teachers at Kirigi School have gone crazy over this new American. She has been here only one week and already they have given her an African name: *Makena*, meaning *one who laughs*.

Priscilla reaches a sandy Y in the road, turns left, and walks past the six homes that comprise her neighborhood. It is a good neighborhood, comfortably middle-class and respectable.

She sees her house, the last one, well-situated on the property that Henry bought soon after their marriage. Her sister Patience is hanging out the wash. Patience senses her approach, looks up squinting against the afternoon sun, and waves a greeting. Priscilla waves back, absent-mindedly checking the hair-clip at the nape of her neck before allowing her hand to fall back to her side.

Patience, Priscilla, Henry...how had it become

fashionable for Kenyans to name their children with European names such as these? And now this American whom they call Makena. Yes, it must be easy for *her* to laugh. Everything is easy in America.

Priscilla must pay this Makena a visit, like it or not. She shoos a chicken with her foot and decides to go first thing in the morning, so as to get it over quickly. She will remain dignified and aloof. She will bring mangoes and bananas, a simple gift of fruit and nothing more.

Mungai

Mungai watches Makena gather her books and leave the classroom. Tomorrow is Saturday. He will bring her some cabbages and show her how to cook them. He knows that American women have expensive machines to help them do their housework, so how will she know how to handle a kerosene stove? She might not even know what it is. Ah, it must be hard for her here in Meru Town. And not only at the material level. She must also be getting tired of the incessant curiosity, of people crowding around, annoying her with the same old questions about her life in America. What kind of car do you drive, what does your house look like and how much did it cost? He wants her to know that he is not like these small-minded village people. With him, she could have a decent and intelligent conversation.

Mungai too is something of a foreigner in Meru Town, a Kikuyu from a neighboring region of Kenya, and he sees this as a natural basis for forming a friendship with Makena. True, he speaks Kimeru so well, and with no accent whatsoever, that the locals often take him for one of their own. But none would be pleased if he asked to marry a Meru girl and this, in the final analysis, makes him feel unwelcome. Of course, he cannot afford to marry anyway, not on his meager teacher's salary. Ah! If only he could have landed a teaching job in Nairobi, where people are better educated and more open-minded. It would have paid better as well.

He shakes his head morosely and begins to leaf through a thick stack of ungraded homework. I will never be a true member of this community, he thinks, so why *not* befriend a lonely American?

Mama Njoki

On Saturday morning I come to Makena's compound early, bananas in hand. It is not yet 8:00, but Joseph tells me that she has already gone out. *Eh?* Gone to the market on her own two feet, even knowing that they will try to cheat her?

I sit down in the shade, on the wooden bench that Joseph keeps in front of his shop, and Joseph begins to complain. "Mama Njoki," he says, "this Makena is forever going to and fro, trying this, looking at that..." And every time she leaves the compound, he must remind her to lock her room, as if she were a small child. "But she is friendly," he says, "always laughing." And I can see that Joseph likes Makena very well indeed.

He is telling me that he saw her washing clothes in a plastic bucket with her own two hands when a young man arrives with a sack full of cabbages. It is Mungai, the young Kikuyu who came to teach here just last year.

"She is not at home," Joseph calls out, certain that Mungai has come to see Makena.

Mungai looks disappointed, but greets me correctly, and with a smile. *Eh!* This one has not forgotten how to show respect to his elders. Not like so many boys nowadays. I return Mungai's greeting with pleasure, then say to Joseph,

"Tell Makena that Mama Njoki was here to see her." I give him my bananas and I go my way.

As I approach the jacaranda tree that marks my turning, I decide to go a little farther and pay a visit to Priscilla. Her house is not far. But before I have taken five more steps, I see Priscilla coming up the road. She is wearing her nicest dress and carrying a small bundle of fruit and *eh!* I know where she is going.

Mungai

Mungai sits down in the place deserted by Mama Njoki, commenting to Joseph that these are most unusual circumstances for a *muzungu*. A small compound such as this, with no electricity and no running water? Even Peace Corps workers get better than that.

He checks his watch. Nine-thirty and already the day is growing hot.

Joseph informs Mungai that Makena has gone to the market. Alone.

"That is not at all wise," Mungai says. "Every vendor in the market will try to cheat her. Why didn't you send someone to accompany her?"

"What makes you think I had any say in the matter? I have trouble enough to make her lock her door when she leaves."

"Tell me Joseph, it is true that she has no money?"

Before they can pursue this topic any further, Priscilla steps up out of nowhere and Mungai jumps up to offer her a seat in the shade.

"Mama Njoki warned me that I might not be the only one visiting," Priscilla says, not wishing to even pronounce the name *Makena*.

"Oh, I was just passing by," Mungai replies.

Priscilla

Priscilla sees the cabbage in Mungai's hand and guesses it is a gift for Makena. She is not happy to see Mungai because she had hoped to keep her visit a discreet one, and she also does not want to become any further involved in the ceaseless excitement over Makena.

"Just passing by" indeed. Why would Mungai bother to lie about his visit? After all, he is a man, isn't he? Free to do as he pleases.

She herself could never dream of such freedom. She has come with a single purpose: to see Makena in private with the hope of determining how to best handle their problem, correctly and without letting the whole world know about it.

She remembers with rancor the day Makena arrived, delivered to her door by a stranger who had been traveling in the same *mutatu*. Imagine! A *muzungu* traveling from Nairobi to Meru in a *mutatu*. Six hours in a death-trap of a vehicle stuffed indecently full of passengers—arm to arm, thigh to thigh and cheek to jowl with whomever destiny decides to throw your way.

Muzungus never travel by *mutatu*, so why would Makena? Priscilla did not necessarily believe Makena's scattered explanation. She said she had been waiting at the airport. Waiting and waiting. She knew no one, and very little about where she was supposed to go, but Henry had promised that a friend would be there to meet her.

Finally, she had called a number Henry had given her, and after two more hours of waiting, a man arrived. It was late and the man seemed very tired. He was polite, embarrassed, and clearly not expecting her. Oh yes, he knew Henry, of course, but he had not heard from him in several years. He was sorry, so sorry, but he was not prepared to receive a guest, especially not an *American* guest. He had no car, his apartment was far away, in a neighborhood that was not nice, and he himself had come to the airport in a *mutatu*. Now what was he supposed to do? She told him that she too was sorry, she was trying to get to Meru Town because Henry had arranged for her to teach there, at Kirigi School. So the man set about finding her a *mutatu* and stayed until he saw the driver stuff her in, wishing her luck as the car pulled away in a cloud of noxious fumes. Fortunately, she was seated next to a kind soul who offered to help her find Priscilla.

And so Makena turned up at Priscilla's door-step, a forlorn apparition out of nowhere, and despite misgivings, Priscilla had invited her in for tea. What else was she to do with the bedraggled-looking *muzungu*?

"Henry said I should come straight to you," Makena had said, guzzling cup after cup of tea as though her life depended on it. "He said you would have an apartment ready for me and that you would introduce me to the headmaster of Kirigi School."

Henry! Sitting on the bench in front of Joseph's shop, Priscilla grinds her teeth, wishing for arms long enough to reach Henry in America. She realizes she is so angry, she has failed to extend the standard greetings to Joseph and Mungai and by now it is too late, so she simply inquires of Mungai, "How are your students?"

"They are not brilliant and they do not work hard enough on their lessons," he answers. "But they are good boys and girls all the same."

"Their parents will soon take them out of school to work the farm," Priscilla says. "They have no motivation to take their studies seriously."

"That is so," Mungai agrees. "Perhaps I would be better off teaching first graders like you."

"I don't think so," Priscilla says. "The pay is even less than yours."

Mungai

Mungai walks home, dragging his heels in the dust and marveling at how badly he had misjudged the situation. When Makena returned from the market, she had immediately shown Mungai and Priscilla to her room and unceremoniously dumped an armful of fresh vegetables—cabbage, green peas, and potatoes—onto a rickety table. She began making tea, lighting the kerosene stove as matter of factly as if she had been using one all her life, and when Mungai asked how much she had paid for the cabbage she quoted a price that was slightly better than what he himself had paid. Furthermore, instead of seeming desperate for Mungai's intelligent conversation, Makena was clearly anxious to see Priscilla. Alone.

To top it all off, the tea was perfect. She had already learned how to make it as all Kenyans do, strong but with a lot of warm milk. "My grandmother—on my mother's side —made her tea exactly the same way," she explained, laughing.

He left as soon as he had drained his cup.

But Priscilla. What a sharp lady. Perhaps even a deep thinker like himself. He would like to have a long and personal conversation with *her*, but...

He wonders why her husband does not come to visit her more often. *Tch!* Life is so unfair. If he had a wife like Priscilla, he would never leave her side.

Priscilla

Six hundred dollars! Priscilla scowls as she walks back home, certain that someone is trying to cheat her. But whether it is Henry or Makena—or worse, Henry *and* Makena—she does not know.

As soon as Mungai departed, Makena raised the question of money. She claimed to have given Henry six hundred dollars to pay for her expenses. Henry had insisted it was necessary to send the money to Priscilla in advance so she could have accommodations ready upon Makena's arrival.

Ha! Priscilla thinks, stomping along the dirt pathway. If I had six hundred dollars, would I be wasting my time fretting about how to house and feed this hapless, ridiculous American?

She had no proof that Makena had given Henry any six hundred dollars, and she certainly had not received any money from Henry. It was going more than a year since he had even called.

It was time to face the possibility that Makena might very well be another of Henry's girlfriends. The last time he came, he had brought two of them. Yes two, and they had stayed in her house as guests for nearly a month.

Priscilla had cooked and cleaned and seen to their needs as any responsible wife must do, yet the girls and Henry hardly bothered to conceal themselves, laughing and embracing one another right in front of her, lolling about on the sofa and letting their arms droop lazily onto the small end table, eventually upsetting the telephone, that horrible instrument of her shame which had failed to ring over the course of two long years. Two years without a word, nothing, while she had struggled to care for her children on the paltry salary of a first-grade teacher and vegetables from the garden.

But at last he had called, telling her not to worry, and at last he had come to visit, arriving with a girl on each arm and introducing them as friends he had made in America.

The worst of it was that Priscilla had never in her life seen Henry in such a jolly mood. With her he had always been stern and reserved, seldom laughing and never, never touching her for the sake of pure joy or affection. But with these two girls he was quite the Romeo. And they were Kenyan girls, not Americans. Students on exchange, Henry said, and when Priscilla asked them about their lives in America they held their hands in front of their faces and giggled, bracelets jangling on their wrists. How she hated them!

Of course it was Henry who had betrayed her, but she had no hope of reckoning with him. She had tried it only once and was astounded at how easily he had defeated her.

Henry I want to know why you never called.

Henry...Henry? Did you hear me? Henry, I want to know what, exactly, you are doing in America.

Henry, you must answer me...These girls...who are they? Why did you bring them here?

Henry sat stiffly, face cast in iron, heart closed like a coffin. He stared past her with such fierce determination that her questions dropped silently, one by one, into the dark void between them and disappeared without a glimmer, without a single consequence. Dry desert sand filled her mouth, preventing further speech. Powerlessness and despair invaded her gut like an army of fiery marching ants, eating her up from the inside out.

Even his own mother, the one who gave him life, had been unable to get a word of sense from him.

When Priscilla passes the large jacaranda that marks the turning to Mama Njoki's house, she pauses for a moment, then turns down the path toward her own home. One thing was becoming clear: the longer she went without answers the more she feared the truth.

Mama Njoki

Eh! Six hundred dollars! Have we lost our minds now? A room in Joseph's compound costs no more than four hundred shillings per month and this amounts to only three or four American dollars. As for food, you could not eat all the potatoes and cabbages that six hundred dollars will buy if you live to be a hundred. Makena can see all of this for herself, so if she is not the one who is cheating Priscilla, she must surely think that Priscilla is cheating her.

Is it not possible that what Makena says is true? That she made arrangements with Henry, who promised to forward the six hundred dollars to Priscilla? What we would expect then is for Priscilla to receive the money and complete her assignment as economically as possible. If there is any surplus, she would be allowed to keep it as payment for her trouble. In this way, a husband can sometimes pass along some money to his family. But now...now the money seems to have disappeared entirely. Much like Henry himself, from whom we have heard nothing since his last visit, when he brought with him two girls and managed to impregnate his wife at the same time! No, no, do not think badly of Priscilla. A wife cannot refuse this duty to her husband under any circumstances, unless she is prepared to withstand the worst abuse.

Tch! We have seen it happen this way before. A husband goes to Europe or America to make his fortune, and once there, loses all sense of decency.

Mungai

Mungai sits up in bed, wondering what he should do. He has heard talk that Priscilla's marriage is over, that her husband has not fulfilled his duties to her in a very long time. It is unjust that such a nice lady should be so terribly unfortunate. It only goes to show how much the happiness of a wife depends on the good humor of her husband. If he treats her badly she has no recourse whatsoever. True, she can leave him, but this takes courage as well as finances and her ability to bargain for another husband is not as good the second time around. And she must remarry, for what good is a woman without a husband to protect her and provide for her? Mungai prides himself on being well above this outmoded fashion of thinking, but one must also face facts.

In Mungai's case the facts are simple. One, owing to his poor salary he is among the most desperate of men in need of a wife. Two, he likes Priscilla very well indeed. From there, it is only a small step to realizing that he should investigate his possibilities with Priscilla further.

But he cannot marry Priscilla! What is he thinking? She is a good fifteen years older than he, with three children and not yet formally divorced from her husband. On the other hand, there is no denying that Priscilla needs a good man and that he needs a good woman. All other concerns are reduced to mere superficiality in the face of such need.

Perhaps they could arrange something...at least until he has more money.

Money. Dear God, if only he could pay the dowry for a bride, a bride of his own...and now Mungai can see her smiling sweetly in his mind's eye. She is young and innocent, she will be completely devoted to him for the rest of her life and Mungai is sure that he will always treat her kindly. His parents could arrange it all tomorrow, with any number of girls from his own home village. If only he had the dowry.

Seeing the girl of his dreams so clearly sobers Mungai's thinking. He reminds himself that he must hold out for the best, for what is rightfully his, at all costs.

He rises to blow out the candle flickering on his desk and settles back into bed. It would not be right, but an arrangement with Priscilla—something very discreet of course—might be just the thing to help him maintain his courage in the face of such a long wait.

Priscilla

Priscilla rises from her bed feeling tired. It is Saturday morning and another restless night has convinced her that her only recourse lies in frank discussion. Determined to get to the bottom of the confusion once and for all, she sends one of her children to Makena's compound, inviting her for tea.

Makena arrives at eleven o'clock, more than a little late, and enters Priscilla's parlor babbling about how she missed her turning, distracted by the large jacaranda trees which are blooming, flowers falling everywhere, blue-purple and so lovely, so wonderful...She is laughing in a way that reminds Priscilla of Henry and his two girls, and for a moment Priscilla wishes that she had never learned to speak English. What gibberish!

When the standard greetings are finished, Priscilla pours the tea. She gathers her courage and speaks. "Excuse me for saying so, but I do not understand what you are doing here. The headmaster assures me that he is not paying you, he says you are a volunteer. I thank God that he was willing to pay the rent on your room and buy your food. It does not cost much, but I have not a shilling to spare. I do not live an easy life here and I cannot imagine why you would want to come to a place like this and work for nothing. I wonder if you have an ulterior motive. I have even asked myself if you are Henry's girlfriend. And I want to make this very clear: if you gave your money to Henry as you say you did, he most certainly did not give it to me."

There. She had said it all. Now why couldn't she talk to Henry like that?

Makena sips her tea without speaking, and most importantly, without laughing. Then she tells Priscilla that she is not Henry's girlfriend, and that she did give him six hundred dollars, in the form of a personal check. She would gladly prove it, but has no records at her disposal. A mutual friend introduced her to Henry—a friend who had been encouraging her to visit Kenya. When he suggested she try teaching as a volunteer in a small town, as an opportunity for cultural exchange, she had become interested. Henry told the friend he would be pleased to set it up, that he had brought Americans to Kenya in this way before. Makena knew her friend to be an honest person, and so assumed that Henry too could be trusted. After all, he was a schoolteacher...

"What about his home life?" Priscilla demands, "Did you see him with two Kenyan girls?"

"Yes," Makena answered. She had been to Henry's apartment and he had come to hers, and in both cases he had been accompanied by two Kenyan girls. He had introduced them as his roommates. They seemed shy and never had much to say, even when asked. "You don't mean to say that..." And then Makena does laugh, which makes Pricilla angry. Until Makena says: "Sorry, but why would two young women want to share a man like Henry?"

Priscilla

Priscilla is alone in her parlor, holding the truth in the palm of her hand like an over- ripe fruit. She bites down, and finds it bitter enough to make her retch. But she cannot afford to waste another minute, she has wasted her whole life already.

She lunges for the phone, shouting "Henry! Henry! Do you hear me, you swine? I haven't the money to call, I don't even have your number, but hear me anyway. There were others I could have married, but my family liked you, and for all the usual reasons. Money. Social standing. Stability. Ha! You have failed me in every possible way."

She jerks the cord from the wall with strength enough to tear the whole house down. And why shouldn't she? She begins to hurl things, an entire shelf of useless bric-a-brac foolishly coveted, a row of framed photographs trying to put a happy face on things. She must destroy it all and begin again. She feels elated, flying high and free if only on the wings of her own destruction. A knock sounds at her door but she does not hear it.

Mungai

Mungai stands at Priscilla's door with a long, graceful branch of the jacaranda balanced lightly against his right shoulder and a bundle of delicious mangoes dangling from his left hand.

He knocks, and waits, but Priscilla does not answer.

He shifts the jacaranda and knocks again, harder this time, and again Priscilla does not answer. Perhaps she is busy. Perhaps she has not heard him.

No matter. He shoos a chicken with his foot and decides to come again another day. After all, he is sure to get what he wants, sooner or later.

ARMADILLO

A moist, rich moon is climbing the midnight sky and Dave is stepping into his garden with a loaded shotgun. He hears something out there…is it the armadillo that's been rooting up his melons and trampling his young snap peas? Having bolted from his bed, he is not yet fully awake. He blinks at the moon and feels the need to urinate. Immediately.

He props his gun against the trunk of a large oak, steps some few feet away, and assumes a classic stance. Had his grandson been there Dave would have said, "Now the trick to doing this at your age is to avoid peeing in your eye. At my age, it's to avoid peeing in your boots." But Dave is alone and so he stands silently, not peeing in his boots, and suddenly an armadillo is scurrying past the oak, knocking the gun to the ground, and before he has time to curse himself for forgetting the safety, the gun fires and blows off half of Dave's left foot.

Mickie jumps out of bed, awakened by the shot. She opens the back door and takes in the whole scene: gun, blood, foot and all. "Dave Myers, dammit to hell!" Then she drives him, fast, to the hospital, wondering why a man who survived World War II without injury should wind up getting shot by an armadillo in his own garden.

Mickie has had experience with people shot and bleeding. In her youth, she was a nurse's aide at the Lavaca County Hospital, which is where she met Dave, shot in the thigh that time—that time so many long years ago.

Dave was twenty then, and newly engaged to a high-society girl. He had just arrived home, on a two-week leave from basic training in the U.S. Army. Corporal David Myers, looking sharp, looking handsome in his crisp Army khakis. Enthusiasm: one hundred plus. Experience and savoir faire: zero minus. A grin that spread from ear to ear.

Dave's fiancée, Miss Leila Miller, had seen to it that the news of their engagement filled the entire social page of the Hallettsville Herald. She had timed the announcement around Dave's leave, so he could escort her to their engagement party, an event that was already the talk of the town. How elegant she would be, leaning lightly on the strong arm of her soldier-in-uniform. She wondered if he would be decorated with those lovely ribbons and medals that make soldiers look so completely dashing. Ribbons or not, she was sure to be the most envied young lady in town, perhaps the whole damn county!

The day that Mickie met Dave, that fragrant spring afternoon, Miss Miller was busy making herself beautiful for the big day. Shopping and sewing, curling and corseting...how would she get it all done in the next two days? Dave was home alone, with time on his hands and nothing special on his mind.

Well what do you know but a couple of his old buddies stopped by to say hello, curious to know whether Dave had been changed by his up-and-coming circumstances.

They called out from the screen door, "Dave Meyers, you sorry son-of-a-bitch!"

"Nothing sorrier than the likes of you two ugly bastards," Dave replied and swung the door wide.

They opened some beers and quickly exhausted the topic of Dave's uniform. "Women go for men in uniform, and that's a fact," the buddies agreed, without looking especially ready to go sign up for anything. After a few more beers and an interlude of listening to flies buzz against the screen door someone says he heard they hired a new whore down at the Lazy J.

Sure enough? Well why not go have a look at her, just to see if she's worth looking at.

Why not.

The next morning there was a small write-up in the Hallettsville Herald stating that David Myers had checked into Lavaca County Hospital due to a gunshot wound suffered during military training, in preparation for important World War II ground maneuvers. The Herald was happy to report that Dave would soon be fine, and they sure were proud of all young soldiers like him.

Miss Miller read the write-up and knew it was a lie. She hunted down the truth, flew into a fury, and called off her caterers, hoping that the Hallettsville Herald would continue to keep the distasteful facts under wraps.

When Mickie entered room #43 to change Dave's bandage, his leg was hurting, but not so much that he neglected to flash her his charming smile. Mickie went right to work, pulling tape, wrapping gauze, and systematically ignoring the way that Dave watched her every move.

Now here is a woman who does not mess around, Dave thought. She knows what she's here to do, and by God, she's going to do it. She smoothed a line of adhesive tape across his thigh with such determination that he was moved to tell her the truth about what happened; how he was shot, how he knew that Miss Leila Miller would be calling off their engagement, and how you just can't change who you really are.

Dave was a man who loved to tell a good story, and as long as it came out funny, he didn't care at all whether it made him look good or bad. He told it well and Mickie listened without comment from start to finish. She had already read the article in the Hallettsville Herald and had already laughed out loud, right along with the whole damn town. Training for ground maneuvers? Everyone and his uncle knew that Corporal Myers had been shot in a whorehouse.

"I guess it had to happen," Dave concluded. "A soldier's uniform can open a lot of doors, but underneath I'll always be a farmer's son. What the hell was I thinking anyway, marrying into a high-class family like the Millers."

"Well at least you're honest," Mickie finally said, and agreed to their first date. As she left to resume her rounds, she turned and said,"One thing I can't stand is a man who lies."

When the war was over, Dave came home and Mickie thanked God for his life. They married and built a house on the farm that belonged to Dave's parents—down the hill from the main house and just south of the black land, where the soil was particularly dark and rich.

They worked hard, the years passed, and Mickie bore a son. They named him David, and Dave called him Butch. Butch grew large and strong and passed easily into his early manhood. When he was twenty, he left the farm to study agriculture at Texas A&M. Every summer he came back smarter and more polite than the summer before. He helped Dave dip the cattle against black flies, and hauled ripe watermelons out of the garden for Mickie.

Through it all Dave never stopped telling his stories. He would tell people how he had walked into the whorehouse with an open beer and the madam had told him that drinking on the premises was not allowed. "Why hell, look around you, I said. All these women are drinking! Drinking beer every one.

"The girls can drink, says the madam, but customers cain't.

"That's not fair, I told her, but she didn't care. Customers cause trouble when they drink.

"Says who? I said, because I didn't want to waste that beer.

"I do! said the madam, and blam! Just like that, she shot me in the leg."

Dave also liked to tell his picket fence story, which had happened before he'd joined the Army and concerned a policeman's wife. He'd been sneaking in and out of their house for a week or so, when one night the policeman came home unexpectedly. "He was a big man with a big gun, and there was nothing for me to do but jump out the back window and run for my life. Two stories up, and damn if I didn't land right beside their picket fence. One slim inch to the right and I would have been skewered like a goddamn pig! My guardian angel was looking out for me that night, lemme tell you."

Mickie wondered aloud if the policeman's wife ever sat around telling the same story to her friends.

"Why hell no! Her husband'd killed her just as quick as he'd a killed me," Dave replied with his eyebrows riding up as if to say what a silly question.

Mickie sighed. "By God, you can believe it when they say it's a man's world. I'm glad I never had a daughter."

One evening, some long-lost relatives stopped by for a visit—the sort of relatives that don't make it out to the country very often—and by the time Mickie was serving the second round of coffee, Dave was telling them about the time he saw his father sneaking off with the widow woman that lived up the road.

"I saw 'em both with my own eyes. Sneaking off to the chicken shack down at the bottom of the hill, next to that big sycamore where we used to bleed the hogs. The old man—my old man!—skulking along in the dark, drunk most likely, and the Widow James right behind him every damn step of the way. Guess you can't blame her much, her husband'd been dead nigh on six or seven years. But the old man…

"He was always up to some sort of foolishness. He drug me off fishing down at The Sandies one time, and after ten minutes of not catching anything he decided we should set some illegal trout lines. I refused, but he handed me one end of the line anyhow.

"Well, he's in the river chest-deep, yelling at me to do this! and do that! when all of a sudden I get this feeling that someone is watching us and damn if it's not a game warden, in uniform and a pistol on his hip. I was sure he'd slap a fine on us, maybe even take us to jail, but leave it to the old man. He just wades out onto the bank, right up to where the game warden is standing, and offers him a drink! Wearing nothing but his hat, mind you!

"So there they are, up on the bank, sipping and laughing and having a fine old time, and me standing out in that cold water like a half-wit, still holding onto my end of the trout line.

"I'll tell you what, ain't nothing more naked than a man wearing just a hat standing next to an armed game warden."

"That hat!" Mickie said. "Beat-up, sweaty, and dropped in too many cow patties. Your Mama was always after him to get a new one."

"Mama." Dave knocked his pipe out and snorted. "Now where in the hell was Mama while the old man was making fast-steps out to the chicken shack? That's what I'd like to know."

Mickie clucked her tongue and wondered why anyone would want to go fooling around in a shack full of chicken shit.

"Never asked about it though," Dave said. "Wasn't raised that way."

Butch married his girlfriend, Pat, and they set up house in a nice neighborhood in Houston. They called Dave and Mickie every Sunday afternoon, and about once a month Pat mailed them a cassette tape.

"Hi there, Mama and Papa Myers," the tape would say, "This is Pat…"

"…and Butch," Butch would chime in.

Mickey was glad that Butch and Pat sounded happy. Recalling the early days of her own marriage, she stopped the tape and said to Dave, "Remember that time we spent more money than we should have on a brand new car?"

"Oh that. Sure I do. Dark blue Ford sedan. First new car we ever had."

Mickie remembered how they had left the car lot, laughing foolishly and bouncing on the cushy new leather seats.

"I wonder how we look in here," she had giggled and Dave had pulled over on the spot. He got out and stood by the side of the road.

"Go on," he had said. "Go on and drive past so I can see how good you look."

⟪⟫

The doctors wanted to amputate the foot, but Dave flatly refused. Too bad, they said, you have no choice. There will be complications. Infections. It was a question of architecture, bearing weight, bearing pain. Circulation. Gangrene. You could die, or lose the whole leg.

"It's my goddamn foot and I'm keeping it," Dave said.

"I think he means to keep that foot," Mickie told the doctors.

He had toes and a heel without much in between, but it all healed up somehow, and within a year, Dave was on the go again, clomping around in a big boot stuffed with rags to fill in for what was missing.

But why should a man who survived World War II end up getting shot by an armadillo in his own garden? It set Dave to thinking, and the next time he saw an armadillo scurry through his garden, he trapped it for investigation.

He named the armadillo Horowitz, after his commanding officer, and fashioned it a nest from a wooden box that he lined with twigs, leaves and an old red plaid nightshirt.

Horowitz slept most of the day, hunkered down on the red plaid, under Dave's side of the bed. Mickie said it smelled and Dave suggested she pick flowers for her side of the bed—if she wanted to.

In the evenings, Dave took Horowitz out to forage. Together they burrowed between Dave's tomatoes, around his green beans and under his sweet potato vines, looking for caterpillars, worms, beetles and other creatures that mean dinner to an armadillo. If Horowitz made the mistake of trampling on anything Dave would jerk the nylon cord that served as a leash and shout, "Goddamn it, Horowitz, stop acting like an idiot!"

And so it came to pass that Dave got so preoccupied with his armadillo that he had no more time for telling stories, and Mickie did not know whether to thank God or call the doctor. She had certainly had her fill of Whorehouse and Picket Fence, but after more than forty years of living with a man who could not shut up about anything, this clomping around in silence was worrisome.

As for Horowitz, he settled into his new life so well that Dave stopped using the leash. As soon as Horowitz smelled the scent of early evening, he and Dave would sashay out the back door and make tracks for the garden. Mickie watched, amazed at how Horowitz had developed the uncanny ability to match his cautious, bumbling gait to Dave's determined clomping. She watched, and made up names for them: Carry On and Make Do, Folly and Happenstance, Fury and Misfortune, Insult and Injury.

While Horowitz hunted, Dave pulled weeds and

philosophized. "People say that the only sure things in life are death and taxes, but I know it's weeds. Look here! Even an armadillo can see that nature is against humans." And shaking a clump of uprooted weeds at Horowitz: "If you can walk around half blind, eating just about anything you bump into, why can't I eat weeds?"

Dave had always known, in general, that armadillos could not see very well, but watching Horowitz stumble around had made him realize it at a far more personal level. The only reason Horowitz had knocked that shotgun over—and by now Dave believed it was indeed Horowitz —was because he'd had no idea in hell that the shotgun was even there.

Dave became fascinated by the fact that a clumsy, blind creature like Horowitz could hold out in a world full of agile and sharp-sighted predators, and the day he saw Horowitz walk straight into a wall, he had a vision of Creation. God was standing on a big tree stump with his arms spread wide, creating the animals. It must have been the fourth or fifth day of Creation, because the earth, the planets, the stars and what-have-you were already there. God made the predators and gave them strength, speed, and cunning. Then He made the prey and gave them clever disguises and the most acute of senses.

"But look at you," Dave said to Horowitz. "A blind bumbling idiot with nothing but a hard shell to protect you? It covers everything—even the tail—but not the soft underbelly."

By now there were grandkids, and when they visited, they liked to chase Horowitz through the house. He would hide under the bed, then lie still and let them touch his shell. If Horowitz bumped into a chair or a wall during the chase, they would giggle and shout, "Go around! Go around!"

"Why doesn't he go around?" they asked Dave.

"He's damn near blind."

"Why?"

"His eyes don't work."

"Why not?"

"You're probably too smart to understand it now, but wait awhile. You'll soon grow up and get stupid like the rest of us, and then you'll be able to."

"Go outside and play now," Mickie said. "Grandpa's teasing you."

"No, I'm not," Dave shouted as they ran out the door. "I'm telling you the truth. But no one wants you to hear it."

Mickie conferred with Butch in private.

"He hardly talks at all anymore, except to that armadillo."

"He's brooding over something."

"If I had any sense, I'd just sit back and enjoy the silence. He might start up again, any day now."

"Any reason why he named it Horowitz?"

"He says a man by the name of Horowitz was his commanding officer in the army. Figure that?"

"No. It's not like him. Not like him at all. I don't remember hearing a single Horowitz story, do you?"

"Nope. Can't say that I do."

At first, Dave had thought Horowitz was a genuinely nice guy. Dave's first two commanding officers had been older and more experienced. Harder. The first one transferred out, and the second one got shit-faced drunk one night, stumbled into a slit-trench latrine, and drowned there. They promoted Horowitz to fill the sudden vacancy and everyone in Dave's division took to him right away.

"Why hell, he wasn't much older than us," Dave said to Horowitz the armadillo. They were in the garden and Horowitz was wriggling under a potato vine. "But he seemed so confident. He talked the talk, and he walked the walk, and we put our trust in him."

Dave looked up from his weeding to check the sky. The sun was a red-hot ball of fire sliding over the edge of the earth, streaking wild swaths of red and orange across placid blue. How could a man ever get enough of that big Texas sky?

Welcoming the cool and calm of evening, which he did not yet feel, Dave turned back to his weeding, and back to spinning his yarn.

"You could say that things were going along just fine—if anything about a war can be described as going along just fine—until we started winning. Then our assignment changed. Our orders were to go into each and every little town and disarm the German citizens. I'm talking about your normal everyday German families. Grandpas, grandmas, moms, kids, aunts and uncles. Everybody but the soldiers we had been fighting the week before. That's when Horowitz started to turn mean.

"We'd go in to search homes for weapons and Horowitz would tell us to tear the place apart, even go out and dig up the garden. These Germans are sneaky, he'd say, and sure enough, we nearly always found something buried in the garden. Might be guns. But usually it was just a ham, or a hunk of cheese. Never mind what it was, Horowitz hated the fact that they'd tried to hide something.

"One day, we went into a house that was full of beautiful furniture and tapestries. Horowitz started smashing the furniture to bits, and the old granddad of the house ran to save a tapestry that was hanging in the parlor. It must have meant something special to him because when Horowitz came over and put a gun to his head, the old man just stood there, blank-faced and holding on to his tapestry for dear life. We were all watching, all of us soldiers and the old man's family too, everyone afraid to move a muscle. 'Let go, you greedy bastard!' Horowitz was shouting. The old man probably didn't understand a word of English, but I'm sure he knew that Horowitz was threatening to blow his head off. He just kept standing there, though, shaking but determined, and finally it became just too much for Horowitz to handle.

"Somebody should have stopped him...*I* should have stopped him! I guess we all thought he wouldn't really do it.

"After we left, about five miles down the road, Horowitz threw the goddamned tapestry out of his jeep, right out in the middle of the road."

Dave, clutching a handful of weeds, looked down at Horowitz. "I am sick to death of everything," he said. "And you too, Horowitz, you blind son-of-a-bitch. All you care about is digging up my garden." He pushed Horowitz away with his boot. "Go dig up someone else's garden for a change."

Mickie awoke and noticed that the bedroom smelled fresh and breezy. She checked under the bed. No Horowitz. No red plaid. She went into the kitchen and Dave handed her a cup of coffee, made exactly the way she liked it, with a half-teaspoon of sugar and a generous splash of cream.

"Where's Horowitz?" she asked.

(◊)

However much Mickie wanted to celebrate the passing of Dave's armadillo phase, she had the uneasy feeling that all was not right. He was still working his garden, still fighting the weeds, but he had started to complain about his body. His back was aching, his knees were grinding, his boots were uncomfortable.

"Well what do you expect, Dave? You just spent three hours working in the garden."

"I'm getting old. "

"It happens."

One day Dave came in from the garden and said his balls were hurting. What now? Mickie thought. That evening, he called her into the bathroom. He was sitting in the tub, legs akimbo, staring at his left testicle, which was swollen to five times its normal size.

"Look," he said, and his voice had a squeaky quality she'd never heard before.

"Oh my. Do you want to go to the doctor?"

"Those knife-happy idiots? Hell no!"

"Well, how about some baking soda in your bath water, then. Maybe it's a tick bite."

"Epsom salts. Epsom salts are good for swelling, aren't they?"

She left, and returned with a large bowl of warm Epsom salt water.

"Pour it right on the damned thing," Dave said. He lifted his testicle carefully out of the water. "Damn, it weighs a ton! Here, hold it. Feel for yourself."

Mickie took the testicle. "Heavy as a cantaloupe!" she exclaimed and began pouring the warm water.

Dave stared at the swollen organ in Mickie's hand, wishing it had nothing to do with him. "I have things on my mind, Mickie. Things I never told you about."

"Something you can't talk about?" she said, pouring steadily. "That is something."

"It's about the war."

"So."

"You can't talk about war with someone who hasn't been in one."

"Well, talk about it or forget about it but don't start whining. It doesn't suit you." She straightened abruptly and dropped the testicle without warning.

"Ouch! Goddammit Mickie! Ouch!" How could she be so inconsiderate?

Mickie stomped out of the bathroom, wondering for the umpteenth time if that Picket Fence business really had happened before he'd met her—as if it really mattered at this stage of the game. The randy old goat. Yet weaker than a child when it came to his balls.

She reminded herself to be glad they still had their chemistry. His pipes were still pumping; not like some men who lost their abilities with age.

But why was he always talking, talking, talking, without actually telling her anything?

Dave's bath water was getting cold but he stayed put. He was thinking about the fact that his own grandfather had been a German immigrant, that Horowitz must have been a Jew, and that it was anybody's guess by now whose long-lost relatives had shot at whom. Some had lived and some had died, this he could accept. What he couldn't stand, or understand, was how it had felt to look another human being in the eye, hoping you'd be able to kill him before he killed you.

Who had ever been able to talk about it truthfully? No one.

It made him wonder if he had ever really told the truth about anything.

All those stories he had told. He had marched them up and down like soldiers on parade, but what did he mean by it all? He saw a caricature of himself jumping out of a bedroom window and realized he did not remember the woman, only the story, told over and over.

Well, he had tried. God knows he had tried. But a man should only go so far. You can lose yourself in a story if you don't watch out.

The swollen testicle quickly returned to normal but Dave's mood continued to deteriorate. Mickie began to dread the nights. He stopped pulling close to share his warmth when they got into bed, and as soon as he fell asleep, he would jerk and mumble and pull the covers completely onto his side; burrow under, get hot, and throw it all off and onto the floor.

The days were worse. He sat before the TV, raging against the politicians in Washington, the army doctors, the bank tellers and the expression on old man Janek's face when they passed each other on the road. He hated them all. He complained about Mickie's cooking, objected to the tone of her voice when she spoke to him, and could not bear the sound of her slippers flopping against the kitchen floor.

Evenings he passed in a determined silence, smoking his pipe and reading accounts of war. If she tried to talk to him, he would snarl, "Leave me in peace! I don't want to talk to you!"

This is no way to live, Mickie thought. She called Butch and asked him to bring the family out for the weekend.

"I know why you're here," Dave said when they arrived. "I heard her call you." He did not let their presence interrupt his bad mood in the slightest.

After dinner, the grandkids asked him for a story and he said, "Story? Go read one of those history books on the shelf over there. Made-up fiction, every one."

As they were leaving, Butch whispered to Mickie, "Come and stay with us whenever you want, you hear? Just say the word and I'll come get you."

Mickie kissed him on the cheek and waved him away. She went inside and plopped down in her rocker, feeling heavy in spite of the fact that she had become quite thin. So many years, so much living, all gone by. She felt tired— unimaginably tired—and at the same time oddly indestructible.

Love should not run out, she thought. But let him do whatever he wants, he can't hurt me. I will be like Mahatma Gandhi. I will survive it all.

Gandhi was dead of course, but Mickie knew that women were naturally blessed with more staying power than men. They had to be.

⟨◊⟩

A few months later, Dave drove to town. He was filling his first prescription for heart medicine and he had to go the new Walmart store because the old pharmacy had closed down. To get to the prescription counter, he had to wind his way through a maze of products that did not interest him. Hair dyes, videos, deodorants, t-shirts, socks, plastic forks, paper plates and—this is the one that really got him—a section called "hardware" lined with packets of tiny screws and nails and hammers that looked like they'd break in half if you so much as touched them. When he finally got to the pharmacy window there was a gigantic plastic fish singing "Don't worry, be happy."

"What the hell is going on in here?" Dave growled. "Is this what you call a pharmacy? Do you think anybody is going to buy any of this crap?"

"Sir, do you have a prescription to fill?" said the young man at the pharmacy window. He wore a gold earring on his left ear and looked as though he had just flown into town on a magic carpet.

The old pharmacy had been a small, friendly place run by the Mikulinka family and situated right across from Ringer's hardware store where they sold real hammers you could build a house with. If Dave had ever yelled at Mr. Mikulinka, Mr. Mikulinka would have yelled right back, "Don't get grouchy with me, Dave Myers. Just because you're getting old."

As he was leaving, the former Miss Leila Miller was coming in. She had married the oldest son of the only lawyer in town, who had succeeded his father, as all good sons must. Leila's corset looked tight as ever, as did her smile. Dave nodded across the divide of their lives, wondering if she was there to fill a prescription too.

That night, he held the bottle of pills up to the lamplight and shook them lightly. "I don't know if I should take these damn things or not," he said to Mickie. "You know how these idiot doctors are. Try to cut off your foot when you need it to walk on, then turn around and try to keep your heart alive when you know it's time to die."

"Well, it's up to you," Mickie said. "But I'd say go ahead and try it."

Dave did not trust himself to answer. After a few minutes he opened the bottle and took one.

His blood pressure went down and his doctors were pleased. They told him to come back for a checkup the next week. And the next. It was important that they see him regularly. They gave him a machine to take home so he could monitor his blood pressure himself, every day. Dave did as he was told, but chafed at the unrelenting supervision of his bodily functions and the never-ending trips to the doctor. Was the pressure up or was the pressure down? Would they increase the dose or decrease the dose? Was he going to live or was he going to die?

"This is stupid," he finally said to Mickie. "Everyone has to die. Why should it be at the beck and call of a bunch of VA doctors who can hardly remember who you are from one visit to the next?"

"Forget about the doctors," Mickie said. "You still have some good years left to spend with your family if you could just accept the fact that life changes as you grow older."

"Changes or diminishes?"

"Dave Myers, if you fool around and die before you have to, I swear I'll redecorate this entire house."

"Mickie! What's wrong with the way it is now?"

"Just letting you know," she said.

His mood worsened. The list of things he hated grew longer, and if Mickie tried to talk to him about it, he put her at the top of his list. He was so busy in his discontent that he seldom found time to shave or get a haircut and in general took on the appearance of a grizzled old bear—

burly and grey, but still, Mickie thought, somehow handsome.

People in town began to treat him with caution. "Watch out for old Dave," they'd say. "He'll bite your head off soon as say good morning."

"Oh that's just Dave," Janek said, "He's been ready to die for a while now, but just hasn't quite gotten around to it yet."

He was in the garden pulling weeds and when he straightened up to rest his back, found himself looking out across a wide field on the southwest edge of his property. It was a clean stretch of prairie that led down to the creek bottom over where old man Janek's property began. A cow raised her head and looked in his direction then stepped along, munching and browsing. A light wind made waves in the tall grass and Dave remembered another field, on another morning, in Germany.

They had marched through the night then hunkered down in a makeshift battery at the onset of a raid. The night had passed slowly in shifting tides of fatigue, hunger, and nerves crackling in response to the steady explosion of bombs. Their thoughts were of mud, gristle and blood; the cracking of bones. But no one was hit that night.

When dawn broke the bombing stopped and with the strangeness of silence settling over them, they crawled out of hiding to discover they were in the middle of a potato field. The bombs had been churning the earth all night and now there they were—a bunch of tired, hungry men in a field of freshly dug potatoes. "It was the best breakfast I ever had," Dave said to no one in particular, then started back to the house for his pills.

With the bottle held loosely in his right hand, he walked laboriously back out onto the prairie, limping along until he reached what he judged to be the exact center. He stopped, waiting for his breathing to slow. The waves of silvery grass were sweeping him along, rolling right through him. He waited for a prayer but nothing would come. He opened the bottle and raised his arm, then stopped. What if the cows ate them? God only knows what they would do to a healthy animal. He recapped the bottle, cursing himself and the ruination of the moment.

When he got to the house he did not wait for his breathing to settle or anything else. He went directly into the bathroom, dumped the pills in the toilet and flushed. Straightening, he watched the swirl of pills, flecks of blue and white in a silvery vortex of water, twinkling just a little as they passed from his sight.

CRACKING THE CODE

The first time Nina's husband, Mark, proposed the wellness retreat, she flatly refused. "There is nothing wrong with me," she said. "I'm getting older, but I am not unwell."

She was sixty-five yet still running around, deemed by her doctors to be fit, and also exuding the ever-important "youthful spirit." Her brain was still charging along too. Knowing so much—too much really—yet still not enough.

For example: as a retired biologist, she knew that inside her body, the macrophages that had always been at work—the cleanup cells that used to be her friends—were sometimes turning against her, attacking the very tissues they normally protected. Gathering in dank, out-of-the-way places to help enemy cells grow into tumors. Inflaming her joints, clogging her brain with plaques, and so forth. It was all part of the normal aging process, and a preamble to death. A long preamble if you were lucky.

Mark was fifty-three. He didn't know much about aging, yet.

But he'd just been kicked off the elite marketing team at LifeTech—where he'd worked for twenty years—and was taking it badly. Like all such biotech companies, LifeTech thrived on keeping a young face. It was part of their mythology. So Mark was sleeping in, moping around, zombifying in the bluish glare of his laptop. Applying for jobs but not getting any interviews. She'd even caught him injecting himself with something, and when she asked what it was, he said it was a new herbal-pharmaceutical blend to protect his prostate.

She worried it was some bogus male steroid that he'd ordered online. Men did these things, in the same way that women used Botox.

They had married when she was forty-five and he thirty-three, and even though she had always been "young for her age" she knew she would be the one to grow old first, and had wondered how they would handle it. She had expected to feel pressure to stay young for him. But she didn't.

"I feel fine," she is saying to him now. "I work out three times a week. I don't need anything."

He sighs and gives her a hangdog look. "You didn't even read the brochure."

"It's probably just another self-improvement scheme, targeting women and their hard-earned money."

"You're impossible," he says. "Why does everything have to be passed through your feminist filter?"

"Because it's not a filter. It's reality."

He sighs but says nothing.

"Let the marketers pick on men for a change," she says. "What's good for the goose is good for the gander, walk a mile in my shoes…"

"C'mon," he says, voice softening. "You know I agree with you about all that. What's good for the goose *is* good for the gander. That's why I want us to go together."

Well, she thinks. He's buttering me up for sure. But there was no denying he needed a boost. He was the one feeling old. His ego had taken a beating, and if he needed her company to make the wellness retreat feel less about him, so be it.

"Ok, let's try it," she says, hoping it wouldn't be too awful, hoping it would lift his mood.

⊘

A guard checks their photo IDs against their faces. A valet takes the keys to their car, and asks for their cell phones so they can "completely disconnect."

"I'm a grownup," Nina says, holding on to hers. "I can turn this thing off when I want to." The valet smiles knowingly, as if to say: "Of course you are, but your husband is a techie and techies are *so* hopeless." Nina answers this with a stony stare but hands him her phone.

A porter has appeared at Mark's elbow, and is loading their bags onto a cart. "Why not have a look around," the porter suggests, "before going to your room? Our garden is full of topnotch desert exotics."

"Good idea," Nina says. She had enjoyed studying the desert landscapes as Mark drove, but by now she is stiff from sitting so long.

The porter directs them to a crushed granite footpath and they follow its perfectly tended curves and turnings, hearing nothing but the soft crunch of their own footsteps. The air is pure and still. They wind through aloe vera plants which tower above them, flower spikes so thickly clustered with oblate gold petals that they seem at once ethereal and dinosaur-tough. A few more steps bring them to a mantle of purple blossoms—a velvety Princess Glory— which in turn cascades onto a low-growing blanket of fiery red cactus flowers. "It's a botanist's heaven," Nina says, and at the same time points to the whipping disappearance of a sand-colored desert snake that Mark wasn't quick enough to notice.

Marks pulls up short. "Poisonous?"

"Couldn't tell. But most snakes would rather avoid you than bite you, so just walk slowly and watch where you put your feet."

To Nina's utter surprise, the next curve in the path opens upon a sleek public square with a modern vibe. Taut triangular sails the color of butter shimmer above terrazzo tiles of sapphire blue. A saxophonist sits comfortably on a tall black chair, playing as if to please himself alone. His horn glints gold in the mid-afternoon sun and the air around him seems to hum with an energy that is at once peaceful and invigorating.

Well, Nina thinks, this is sure not what I expected. She turns to smile at Mark and he grins back. "I told you it would be nice." He touches her arm, leaning in, in that slightly proprietary, manly way that allows her to catch his scent. His animal magnetism.

A waiter in a starched white uniform approaches to announce that refreshments are being served, and points to a low-slung building that seems to materialize the moment they look for it.

The waiter seats them on a patio with views of desert formations glowing red and gold in the low-slanting afternoon light, then bedazzles them with the unexpected: greens drizzled with first-press oils and artisan cheeses. Kohlrabi lightly stewed in coconut milk. Hand patted, nutrient-dense patties and patés of things they've never heard of. And instead of the vegetable-fruit-juice-calorie-conscious smoothie that Nina is expecting, they get Desert Mojitos with hand-shaved ice, fresh mint and a lot of rum.

"Wow. A health resort that serves alcohol?" Nina says, when the waiter leaves them.

"Incredible," Mark answers. "And who could say no to any of this? It all tastes fantastic."

Nina giggles, swooning. "This rum is going straight to my head. You'd best take us to our room."

"My pleasure," Mark says, with a bright look that Nina hasn't seen on him in a long time. "But give me just a few minutes. I want to make sure we got the room I asked for. It's got a killer view."

They drain their drinks, and Mark accompanies Nina back to the square, still smiling, still flirty, Nina notes with satisfaction.

She looks around the square. A few people have gathered, and they are standing around listening appreciatively to the saxophonist.

"Enjoy the music, hon," Mark says, leaning down to brush Nina's cheek with his lips. "I'll be right back." He pauses with what seems to be a surge of emotion, looking deep into Nina's eyes and making her remember just how long it's been since they felt connected. "Right," she says, "come right back," then releases him with a pang of deferred pleasure.

As she watches him walk away, her body begins to sway to the music. Brubeck's *Take Five*.

She looks around the square. By now eight or nine people are standing around, grooving to the music, but no one is dancing. The saxophonist sounds better than ever.

Nina always wanted to play sax, but her parents had only laughed when she'd asked for lessons. As if reading her thoughts, a young woman standing next to Nina turns and says, "You can play, if you want." She is dressed in a navy blue suit with nautical tones and is holding a clarinet. She offers it to Nina.

"Ha," Nina says, stepping back a little. "I wish I could." She takes a closer look at the young woman and sees that she is in fact a slender young man. "Do you work here?" she asks.

The young man winks then puts the clarinet to his lips and blows, hitting a shrill note that cannot harmonize with the sax, yet it does.

Damn it, I'm drunk, Nina thinks, and giggles.

She looks across the courtyard again, and sees the spiky aloe vera where Mark exited the square. Going to pee, she thinks, always going to pee, then reminds her drunk self: no, he is checking on our room.

Nina can't stop noticing the young saxophonist. His eyes are closed in perfect concentration. He is blowing into his horn, and has no other interest.

She thinks again of Mark, scans the periphery of the courtyard, and suddenly wishes she had gone with him to check on the room. Maybe she could just walk over and try to find him on the path. But there are several pathways and she has no idea which of them would be right. Mark hadn't given her a room number, or anything.

Her eyes return to the place where Mark exited— marked distinctively by one of the gold aloe spikes—and without warning a creature bursts forth into the plaza. It is muscular and wide-horned, with a bull's thick neck and slick hide, yet propelled by the powerful legs and sweeping claws of a fully grown, fully enraged Kodiak bear.

Crushing the aloe, trampling the flowers, it is lunging straight toward Nina.

Nina recognizes the telltale signs of genetic engineering, but has no time to think about that now. The beast is moving fast, hoof-claws grinding on the grainy concrete, ropes of snot and saliva swinging from its muzzle.

The clarinet player lowers his horn and hands her something, smooth and heavy. A cylinder of some sort. Then he steps back, joining the small crowd of onlookers. They move aside, leaving Nina to stand alone.

"Hit it!" someone screams.

Hell no, Nina thinks. The thing is ten times bigger than me. Why don't *you* hit it? She tries to make eye contact with the clarinet player, or one of the others, but they are stone-faced and rigid. They don't even look that much like people anymore.

Is there something wrong with her brain?

Nina feels herself expand and contract, expand and contract, yet with a supreme awareness of everything around her. She is frozen, yet racing. Fast, yet slow. Nina's scientist's mind knows that this is a normal reaction to adrenalin and fear, but her animal brain is taking charge now and all it can say is *danger, danger, danger.*

The beast hurtles across the plaza, bearing down on Nina with all of its wild energy and she feels her body going limp. Collapse and play dead? Yes, that could be her best chance. Bears will sometimes maul their prey, then walk away, provided the prey shows no resistance.

But something else begins to happen. Although she does not realize it, Nina's right hand is tightening around the cylinder. She is planting her feet wide and drawing her core muscles tight. She is clenching her jaw and baring her teeth with primitive animal intent. Never has she been less aware of herself or more fully present. Never has she bored into anything with her attention as she does now, pinning the bull-bear like a target, splaying it into components: size, smell, speed; length of stride and thickness of hide; teeth, claws, and glint of eyes. Each of these components carries a message to Nina and the message is: You cannot win. But fight.

When the beast is so close she can smell its rich wet breath, Nina knows the moment has come. She raises the cylinder high above her head and brings it down with all her might, bashing the bull-bear across its unexpectedly soft and lovely-looking muzzle.

She feels the blow connect. Shock waves tear up her forearm, collide in her shoulder joint. A final crush of cartilage and bone, and the bull-bear goes down.

It lies at Nina's feet, quivering and rasping out its final breaths.

Her hand, still locked around the cylinder, is slick with snot and blood.

A man steps up, grabs her by the arm and says, "This way."

⟨⟩

The convertible Mark drives is cherry red—windows down, top down, and wide open to the desert air. It is speeding across flat desert, kicking up a monstrous rooster tail of dust and Mark feels deliriously happy. His left hand feels relaxed yet masterful on the leather-laced steering wheel. His right hand strokes a smooth bare knee. The knee buzzes with vitality. His hand sizzles with expectation.

His hand. Her knee. The excitement and promise of more.

So much more.

It is truth, and self-evident, that he has made the right decision.

Mark's passenger is a beautiful young woman with a ready smile. The kind of woman who lets the wind whip her blunt-cut shiny hair so hard it slaps her face and stings her eyes. The kind of woman who makes him feel like a man.

He cannot tell where the bare knee ends and his hand begins, and this electrifies him with pleasure.

The skirt is short, red, and taut. Smooth, like his upholstery.

He fingers the edge of the skirt, testing its give, then slides his hand farther along, to stroke the inner thigh. The smooth woman thigh, welcoming, pulling him in, life seeking life, ancient and unfettered.

Preposterously, and with all of her characteristic abruptness, Nina's spirit looms upon the scene, invading Mark's consciousness and destroying the moment. "No!" he hisses at her. "Move along. Get lost."

He must banish her, yet…who but Nina could share his appreciation of how the tawny leather upholstery provides perfect counterbalance to the gleaming cherry of the car? How it adds just the right note of intelligence and control to the wildness and freedom of red? Yes, he and Nina have always seen eye to eye on such things. Always agreed on art, decor, the finer points of things.

Nina interrupts his thoughts with a sneer. *"A blonde and a red convertible? How creative."*

Oh fuck you, Nina, Ms. Scientist, you smart aleck, know-it-all sarcastic bitch. Did no one ever teach you to play the fucking game once in a goddamned while?

Obviously not.

After twenty years of marriage to a woman like Nina, there wasn't a man alive who wouldn't strike back to save his pride.

And hadn't Nina always claimed she wanted to go fast when the time came, doing something she loved, like hiking or skiing or rock-climbing? Wasn't *that* a cliche? Why should he support her cliche and be denied his?

No point regretting anything now. It was the way of the world and LifeTech had him by the balls. He had no choice.

"Bullshit!" Nina springs right back at him, raking and clawing and spitting. "You're setting me up to die like some misplaced, amateur matador in an Arizona health resort!"

And at this Mark can only sigh.

෴

Again, the man who looks like Jack Nicholson tugs gently at Nina's arm and again Nina rocks back slightly, trying to get a better look at his face. He is old, and unutterably odd.

But also, *she* is odd—wobbly, yet still super-charged from her encounter with the bull-bear, and trembling with post-peak adrenalin. She does not know what to make of this man with the Jack Nicholson smile.

He hands her a foamy drink that she knows will taste like velvet.

She takes a big gulp and they walk together down a curving flight of stairs to the edge of a pool where all is quiet, save the trickle of a drain. The water is calm, and seems to stretch on and on, forever, world without end, amen.

Nina gulps the drink again, throws off her clothes and dives headlong into the pool.

The water is silky and soothes her instantly.

She begins swimming in her usual style, at once vigorous and methodical, feeling free and good. But just as she begins to settle into a sense of wellbeing, to believe that everything will somehow be set to rights, an obese male figure swims past with a disapproving air.

Disapproving what? Her age and nudity? Probably, the ugly old warthog.

Will she never be left in peace?

Never mind, it is time to get out. She needs to find Jack.

No! She needs to find *Mark*.

Laying both palms flat on the smooth edge of the pool, she thrusts herself up and out of the water with a single supple motion, like a dolphin, confident in her strength and balance. As she straightens, water cascades from her body, coursing warmly down her back and legs. She slicks her hair. Grabs a thick white towel perfectly folded on a slatted wooden bench. Wraps her body then takes a second towel for her hair.

Her clothes are gone, but in their place a set of stiff cotton whites. Pants, shirt, and a cloth belt; like a karate outfit. She puts them on.

No shoes, but she's fine going barefoot.

Jack reappears, as though from shadows. She studies his face. Wrinkled yet tight. Revealing nothing. "Where is my husband?" she demands.

Jack grins, raises a bony finger to his lips as if to shush her, then cocks it, beckoning her to follow.

He is utterly distasteful. Yet she follows, spellbound.

Mark's fun break is over. The red convertible has been parked, his blonde returned to her B-hive, and his wrist device is signaling the daily Status Report Meeting with a tone that screeches up his spine.

He hates these meetings, hates all meetings, yet the meetings only multiply.

He walks faster, down a corridor with a bunker-like feel, and into the meeting room. He takes a seat at the third-tier table, feeling the paunch of his middle-aged belly strain against his belt, telling himself he will exercise and get in shape. Other programmers and systems architects arrive and take their seats too. Within less than a minute, they are all present, and on time.

Three more minutes and the bio-hackers come striding in, young and lean, staring down at pods, pads and phones as they walk, taking calls and texting at the same time. They spread out randomly, taking seats at the first-tier table. They hunch their shoulders, shrink into hoodies, and stare into their own palms; showing how busy they are; how productive and super-intelligent, with their myriad, counter-cool ways of being cool.

Mark has had a belly full of these little shit-shows by now but the bio-hackers purr with contentment. They are in their element, ready to strut their stuff. They believe in happy endings, and that happy endings can be made to come fast. It's a question of defying entropy, and what could be cooler than that?

As Mark and all of the rest them well know, the top players now are men who made gobs of money doing Internet things then founded their own health-care hedge funds. Now, they are rich enough to fund their own research. The U.S. Government and the European Union and public universities around the world from here to asbestos-infinity can kiss each other's shabby little asses into eternity. Public universities are institutionalized blobs of self-perpetuating hubris; slow and clumsy. Forget them. It's the bio-hackers who are getting things done, making things happen, and yes, they are moving fast.

Mistakes will be made, but what hard-working scientist doesn't break a few test tubes along the way? The game is on, and LifeTech players are going full throttle. One of the younger ones, Sparrow Ass, is a perfect example. After six months of studying human growth hormone in rats, after finding too many roadblocks to experimenting on humans, Sparrow Ass realized he could simply experiment on himself. After his first injection of HGH, he felt so strong he picked up a refrigerator just for fun and busted two vertebrae. Two months later, he injected again, got on his bike and reached eighty miles an hour on a flat straightaway in Davis, California. When his front tire rolled over a bottle cap, the bike went down and Sparrow Ass landed in a ditch with three broken fingers and a crushed ankle. No really. He fucking did it, and he doesn't care if anyone believes him or not.

He is a free agent. Free to make money, free to experiment on himself, and of course he wants others to join him. "Our genome is mapped, we're cracking the code, and if you can crack it, you can hack it."

For bio-hackers, death is a technical problem, and technical problems can be solved. Thermodynamically, it is possible. Which means it is possible.

Forget that crappy old cyborg stuff where you try to keep a man's brain alive in a robot. A man's body is his castle, and his castle can be made indestructible.

People will thank them in the end. Of this they are certain. Because who wants to get old and die? No one.

⟨◊⟩

Nina follows Jack down a long, silent corridor and they enter what seems to be a carpeted apartment.

An elderly woman—small, fluffy and quiet—is sleeping in a single-sized bed. Everything in the apartment is extremely plush, and decorated in shades of red and gold.

Jack shoots Nina a look with his intense eyes and again puts a finger to his lips, even though she's not talking. Everything is perfectly quiet and the room is humming, but silently. He points to a spot on the wall and Nina notices the old-fashioned wallpaper, a swirly pattern in fuzzy red. Like something in a bordello, she thinks, even though she's never been in a bordello. She realizes with a shock that the woman in the bed is dying and quiets herself in every way. She was already not talking but now she hardly breathes.

Jack pushes gently on the place in the wall and it opens.

A secret door!

Oh, this man knows all the tricks.

Nina is struck with a sudden urge to trust him, to tell him about the macrophages in her body—in everyone's bodies—and to ask him if he knows that rich techies in Silicon Valley are on a self-funded quest to discover eternal life—or as they put it "a cure for death." Some of Mark's associates at LifeTech are heavily invested. He'd told her about it.

Of course their formula would only be available to the select few. The techies themselves, and those able to pay.

She studies Jack more closely. More than ever, she feels

driven to start a conversation but is sure he won't want to discuss macrophages with some random "older woman," even though he's the one who is older.

Plus, he gave her that drink at the pool. Suspicious.

She doesn't feel drunk anymore, yet knows she is being pulled deeper, into something.

Jack touches her elbow and they step into in a white room that feels like feathers.

She turns to face him, demanding. "What did I drink?"

He fixes her with a crazed smile, looking mean and friendly at the same time. "Your husband wasn't lying," he says. "This *is* a wellness retreat, but it's for the wellness of younger generations, not yours."

The wellness of younger generations, not yours.

The words hang in her mind and she follows them, tumbling toward light, sliding onto sound, a chamber of notes, a river of gold, of bodily fluids...Tears?

Ah, she thinks, ah...and lets the information soak in, until she is gob-smacked with the truth. This so-called "retreat" is really just a disposal unit for old people, and Jack is their house flunky, working to buy his own shriveling body a little more time in the system. The techno-weenies must have learned something about keeping their macrophages friendly, and Jack signed on to be one of their experimental bodies.

And Mark...those injections. Had he signed on too? Turned her over in return for the possibility of extending his own middle-aged life?

Still certain that the bull-bear was an experiment in genetic modification, she wonders if it escaped from their laboratory. Or was it a staged encounter, meant to crank her up on adrenalin?

Had Mark helped them? Advised them?

Twenty years of marriage, and this is what it comes to?

That's why they took her phone, the bastards. No way to communicate. A tragic accident.

(b)

There was nothing Mark could do to change the path that LifeTech was taking. His only choice was whether to come along, or be left behind to wither. Middle-aged men run out of choices, in tech, in life. He had nowhere else to go.

Rent a car, rent a babe. Keep your job. A man does what a man has to do. It's a simple matter of recognizing and accepting a situation that you can't change.

People like Nina, who believe in the natural cycles of life, who have what they believe is integrity, are bound to die, and they have to die of something. At least he'd arranged for her to go out with a bang, flying high on adrenalin and fighting all the way. Because that was Nina: feisty. And that kind of feistiness? Well. it had to mean the end of her. It was fitting and right. Right and inevitable.

We each have our paths to follow.

Once, our paths were one. Now they diverge. Oh how they diverge.

Mark likes the way he feels with the blonde. *Needs* it. God Almighty, the mere glance of her shaves five years off of his age. The goofy laughter, that feeling of fun.

The blonde makes him feel like a man. A *man*, goddammit.

He is sick of Nina and her independent, free-thinking spirit. Tired of her intelligence and practicality because dammit there are limits to what a man can take. She was older, wiser and knew her own heart, but he...he was stuck in an unprecedented middle age crisis and had an extraordinary chance for something more. Nina had no idea what it meant—what it took—to be a man. To be a winner.

Eternal life, eternal youth? Tithonus, Asclepius, Achilles. The stories have never ended well. Yet the quest continues, and now, if LifeTech still wanted him, Mark had to try. Even knowing full-well that, aside from the founding billionaires, there are now only two men left in the company over 50: himself, and Jack. What kind of long-term role would either of them have, regardless of what they had been promised?

How could he have believed that LifeTech really planned to keep him on as a valued part of their fabulous age-free future?

In her final moments of consciousness, Nina yearns to recoil from Jack, to jerk her arm from his grasp, yet she cannot. He is leading her, slowly and carefully, toward a narrow single bed. She hates the bed, hates the fluorescent lights glaring down onto stark white sheets and a pillow that looks professionally fluffed.

Jack helps her lie down, adjusting the pillow in a way that Nina knows would be uncomfortable if she could still feel her neck.

She tumbles further into velvet, and her good, scientist brain issues a final report on what lies ahead:

Your heart will stop pumping.

Your lungs will stop oxygenating your blood.

You will lose consciousness and die.

The macrophages, glutted with your tissues, having

finished their purpose, will also die.

The bacteria in your intestines, having faithfully digested your food, will spill through leaky cell membranes and putrefy your organs, muscles and skin.

The worms and the ants will crawl onto and into you.

You will dissolve into your elemental components, and scatter across the earth, and through the universe, as fragments of life and non-life.

The desert will sigh and inhale your molecules. The wind will rise up, circulating your molecules through the atmosphere, then pushing them away, to scatter and rejoin the universe, timeless and unbound.

Mark also expects LifeTech to incinerate Nina's body, to release her back into her elements. But they are not going to do that for Nina. They will keep her alive, using her cells as long as they can, a living experiment.

LifeTech holds the keys to the building blocks of life. They can manipulate genes, as well as the "gene influencers," and their purpose is singular: to tweak the macrophages and keep them working, as if servicing a twenty-year-old body.

For LifeTech, Nina remains technically, biologically, and somatically alive, and she will provide them with the same reliable, predictable line of cells to tweak and re-tweak, until they get it right.

This will no doubt take a while...and Nina will live on.

If not forever, almost.

MAN OF LARGE OBJECTS

His real name was Eric but I'll always remember him as the man of large objects. I met him at UT Austin when I was working for the Department of Transportation Engineering—one of those hang-on-by-your-fingernails kind of jobs of which I've had so many. Eric was our secretary and could type 95 wpm, no mistakes.

TOTS—the Texas Office of Traffic Safety—had hired us to analyze accident statistics for their annual Traffic Safety Report. Which is to say they needed some university-jerko types to demonstrate that the highways they were building across the vast and silent prairies of Texas were not in any way deadly. Au contraire! TOTS saw their highways more like a charming network of lace doilies, something that your own grandmother would crochet, and all of it generously nurtured with federal monies.

The Department of Transportation Engineering was small, and the fat new contract meant rush recruiting from other university departments. They put me in charge of bicycle and pedestrian accidents, I guess because I was an out-of-work biologist who could not afford a car. My colleague Elizabeth reigned like a queen over accidents that were related to the use and abuse of alcohol. She had heftier degrees than I did—an M.A. in sociology and a PhD in psychiatry—but was similarly unable to find work in her field. To offset any boredom or frustration she might encounter as a result of wasting her education, Elizabeth pursued a diversity of activities and passions: writing gory tales of ghosts and murder, studying Jungian symbolism, and swallowing small quantities of LSD out at Lake Travis. She was a single mom with two kids, one a mathematical genius and the other begging to drop out of school to become a hairdresser.

I went skinny-dipping with her out at the lake once, a female solidarity sort of outing, and there she informed me that I was a reincarnated dolphin, or maybe a mermaid.

"Dolphin would better," she said. "Dolphins are sleek, lively and free. Most importantly, they are real. Mermaids are pure male fantasy. Sad, attractive creatures with no legs for escaping the very men who invented them."

"Couldn't they swim away with their big tail flippers?"

"It's symbolism," she said. "Mermaids aren't real."

"Then dolphin *would* be better."

"People who derive from aquatic beings are usually good coworkers. That's probably why I find you so easy to work with.

"And by the way," she continued, "I can't stand working with Eric."

"Oh really? I thought you would enjoy having a male secretary. You know, role-reversing, turning the tables and so on."

"No! Eric gives me the creeps!" she said. "I think he might be a reincarnated executioner...an artisan of medieval torture..."

"Eric?" I tried to conjure up an image of him, creepy or otherwise, but the only thing that appeared was a big brownish blob.

Not long after our afternoon at Lake Travis, Elizabeth told me she'd heard that Eric had his PhD in History.

"Specialty medieval?" I joked.

"No doubt," Elizabeth said.

Since I was more tuned into this life than past lives, the news of Eric's degree only made me think of him as another one of "us." Another over-educated, non-gainfully employed graduate. Now, the sight of him at his typewriter —sweating and fretting and peering and grimacing—put me in mind of a flustered chemist cooking pizza for a living.

I started feeling sorry for him.

He started "making comments."

"Two hundred and fifty-four counties in the state of Texas! Do you know how hard it is to lay out tables with *two hundred and fifty four columns*?" Or:

"You know, you got a couple of counties here...probably only about 10 or 12 people all total even living in these God-forsaken places. Kill one pedestrian in a place like that and it's gonna look like a 10 percent mortality rate. How 'bout I just skip over those guys?"

He was a large man, more than six feet and 200 pounds, with a florid complexion that reddened at the slightest exertion, even animated conversation. He had a wild, scattered air about him, and every time I passed his desk, he seemed set on detaining me. Irritating me.

"You know, most folks don't give a sniff about these bike lanes you love so much. They'd rather have more space for their cars."

They probably would, I thought, but didn't say anything because it seemed like all Eric wanted to do was get me to stand around talking.

"It takes all kinds," I said, sounding exactly like my mother.

One day I handed Eric some *deaths according to time of day* data and he said, "Wait. Stop. I need to know how you really feel about your data. About your job. About me."

Bingo. I hated all three! And I was done with Eric and his stupid comments.

"Just type the fucking report, Eric! Type the fucking report and shut the fuck up with your stupid fucking small-talk!"

Was that *me*, banging my fist on Eric's desk so hard that all his paper clips hopped out of their clear plastic boxes?

Eric was irrefutably and irreversibly impressed.

"You are SO strong!" he purred. His eyes began to bulge and water at the same time.

Realizing that he was thinking about black boots and a leather bodice, I felt adrenalin squirting through my veins. My head pounded, and all my tiny body hairs stood on end. Eric and leather? *Run! Run for your life!*

"Well, it serves you right," my mother said. "Such language."

The next day, Eric brought me something.

"What's this?" I asked, approaching my desk.

"It's from Eric," Elizabeth said. She was wearing her objective scientist expression and belied herself only by snorting slightly when pronouncing Eric's name.

It was a 75-pound chunk of quartz, white, opaque and beautiful. It was huge and it was sitting in the middle of my desk, covering all my papers. I picked it up, grunting, and right on cue, Eric came rushing into the room with his wispy brown hair sticking up all over his head as if he had just grabbed a live wire.

"Oh! Let me help you! I know you're strong but..."

"Got it," I gasped and nearly dropped the damned thing on my toe as I heaved it onto the floor.

"Do you like it?" he said. "I found it out at Lake Travis last year, and..." He fidgeted and fumbled, at a loss for words.

It was a geological artifact of extreme beauty. An intrusion and an act of trespassing.

"It's...ah...very large," I said, not wanting him to know I thought it beautiful.

"I can help you carry it home," he said. "It's pretty heavy, as you know."

"No, no thanks. I can manage."

"I thought you might want to use it as a door-stop."

The following Saturday morning, I was humming a tune and doing my dishes while looking out at the big pecan tree in my backyard when I noticed my back gate opening. Hesitantly at first, then wide...wider...wide...and there was Eric. T*a! daaa!* With a cast-iron bathtub on his back. He was bent double under its weight, creeping slowly and inexorably into my backyard.

Was he crazy, carrying a bathtub around on his back as if it were a canoe?

Oh, man of large objects, strange creature who creeps slowly. Patient. Persistent. Long- suffering.

It was difficult—and terrifying—to watch.

The tub's elegant claw feet clutched at the blue Texas sky as Eric proceeded. He huffed and he puffed and was soon close enough for me to see his face, flaming red beneath the white porcelain rim of the tub.

Heart attack! I thought and became livid myself at the thought of Eric dropping dead in my backyard. A glass slipped from my soapy hands. I swore as it shattered, and bolted out the back door.

"Eric put that down right now!"

"Oh, hi there..." Grunting. "Where would you like it?"

"It's a *bathtub*."

"How about over here by your vegetables? You can splash around in it when you're working in the garden. When you get hot..." His face quivered and sweat dripped from his jawline.

I didn't have an answer for that, and he took my silence as permission to put the bathtub down by my vegetables.

It was morning, but the heat of the day was starting to build, and we both stood blankly, sweating.

He was still beet red and trembly, and I feared my mother would try to make me offer him a glass of cold water, but she kept quiet.

"I think you better go home and take a few aspirins or something," I finally said, remembering my mother giving our dog an aspirin to calm him when the neighboring female came in heat.

Eric shot me a lunatic look, with the unblinking eyes and fixated brain of a fly.

"Every four hours," I said, and ushered him out the back gate. Shoo-fly, shoo! You are a reincarnated *drosophilus* and nothing more!

When I was certain he was gone, I went inside and started cleaning up the broken glass.

I had given the chunk of quartz to my friends Diane and Jim, who were starting a rock and cactus garden. They put it next to their tall spiky Sauguro and it looked just great.

But what would I do with this tub?

It sat around in the backyard all afternoon, with its elegant claw feet sunk deep into my lush green grass, cool new blades tickling its big cast-iron under-belly.

The squirrels found it an outrage.

They chittered and chattered and scolded the tub, at first from a distance, then gradually gained the courage to approach and attack. Charging wildly for its nether reaches, two of them scooted idiotically beneath the tub, and emerged unscathed from its other side.

A second pair mounted a direct attack, leaping fearlessly into the tub from one of the pecan's lower branches. Ha! getting in was so easy! But getting out would be another story. The sides of the tub were too slippery to scale, and just a little too high to hop over. In the desperate flailing that ensued, the tub seemed to fill and bubble with squirrels.

What to do but fill it with water and let them spill out...

Once the squirrels had escaped, I looked at the tub, becalmed but full of water and fur. Why not rinse it out, hop in and have a little splash myself? Yes, splishing and splashing and...

And if Eric showed up?

I turned on my heel and went back into the house, feeling creepy. Clearly, the tub must go. I would hire someone to haul it off tomorrow.

The next weekend I went camping with Jim and Diane. We came back late Sunday evening, happy, tired, and a little sun-burnt.

"Hey, what's this?" Jim said climbing up the steps to my front porch.

"Shit!"

"Looks like your man of large objects was here," Diane said.

"Wow, that's solid oak!" Jim exclaimed. "That's a sixteen-foot solid-oak bar with a brass foot rail, just like the one they have down at Old Blind George's. It must be worth a fortune!"

Right. And it was blocking my front door.

The next morning, I stormed into the office, ready for something, I wasn't sure what. Elizabeth was waiting for me with big news.

"Our contract's been canceled," she said. "None of us have jobs, as of this morning."

"What?"

"TOTS canceled our contract. They said we weren't being 'firm enough' with the data."

I went in to see my boss and he said he might be able to offer me a few weeks of cleanup work, would I be interested? As an afterthought, he added that support staff would be "relocated throughout other academic departments," meaning that Eric would soon be typing for some other victim while Elizabeth and I would be rudely unemployed.

I pedaled home, wondering what to do. Accept the offer, or make a clean break on the spot? The idea of moving to some nice little state with only six or seven counties began to seem attractive. By the time I turned into my driveway, I was feeling a little better, feeling the old optimistic fatalism about to kick in. My tires crunched on gravel, I looked up, and there was Eric, sitting in a battered Plymouth Valiant. Sitting there in the sun and the ninety-plus heat. The very sight of him tipped me over.

I began shouting before I even got off my bike, before he even got out of his car.

"Eric, get that goddamned bar out from in front of my goddamned door! Get it out of here entirely!"

He clambered out of his car, grinning. "I came to say good-bye." His grin faded. He gulped, swallowing air.

"I might not be going anywhere," I snapped.

"Well I am," he said. "I'm heading out to Washington, D.C. First thing tomorrow morning."

"Washington?"

"Yeah, it's all over for me here. I don't want to work in any more university offices. I'm sick of the academic scene."

"Well you better not leave till you get that stupid bar out from in front of my door." Did he think I might never want to walk in or out of my front door again?

"I've got an interview with the CIA," he said proudly.

"The CIA?"

"Yes, I think it might be interesting to work for the CIA, don't you?"

"You mean like in some James Bond movie?"

"You never know," he said smugly. "It could prove to be very interesting."

"Well good luck, then, if that's what you want." What the hell. I felt so tired. So worn down by it all. "And Eric, if you could just get that stupid bar out of here..."

"It's not *stupid*," he said. "It was a gift."

"Eric, if you could just move that bar before you go, I sure would appreciate it."

My Mom smiled and applauded.

Ok. Ok. Maybe he wasn't a reincarnated fly after all. But why did Eric's state of being or non-being have to be *my* problem? Did I have no boundaries that must be respected?

I got back on my bike, defeated. I would pedal down to Barton Springs and go for a swim...go relax, cool down...

When I returned, the bar was gone. Easy! *Easy as pie. Easy-peasy.* Where do these expressions come from?

Things always work out for the best.

Do they? How can you tell?

Well, at least I could use my own front door again.

As I carried my bike up onto the porch, I heard a horn toot lightly.

I turned and saw the Plymouth Valiant, dark plumes rising from its exhaust pipes. Eric stuck his head out of the window, I thought he was going to say something, but instead he grabbed the sides of his mouth with both hands and stretched his lips wide, exposing teeth and gums. Then he stuck his tongue out, way out, and waggled it around until I was sure that one of us would gag and vomit.

Was there nothing I could do? Kill him? Help him? Flee from him?

He grinned, shifted into first, and sped glibly away.

Oh man of large objects, strange creature who came to me without warning. Where are the myths to explain the likes of you?

I leaned my bike against the porch railing and went in. Right on in, through my own front door, banging it shut behind me, real loud. Realizing, for the first time, that no matter how hard I worked, or how smart I was, or where I went, there would always be guys like Eric. And someone would expect me to put up with them.

MIRACLE OF THE LLAMA

Have you ever been to Prosper, Texas?

Not many people have.

Prosper is flat and barely above sea level, with dry prairie all around as far as the eye can see or the pickup can drive in a whole day. Some say they wish our prairies were more like the Garabandal high country in Spain, where a famous miracle occurred, but the truth is, everything around here has changed so much we are not sure who we are or what we look like anymore.

As the editor of our paper, the *Prosper Herald*, I've always kept a close watch on everything that happens in this little town. And lately, with all the trouble we've been having, I find myself feeling downright protective.

We were dry dirt farmers until the oil wells came in. Then we got neighborhoods like Panther Creek Estates and people breeding show llamas. Our main breeder, a lady named Margaret, is one of the only two people in Prosper who ever got famous. The other is George, a friend of Margaret's.

In the beginning, when Margaret first started breeding llamas, people would ask *"don't they spit?"* because llamas are related to camels.

Margaret didn't bother to answer. She had seen her first llama on a road trip to Oklahoma and had, as she put it, "jumped in naked." This was how she had lived her whole life, and with few regrets.

The llama's name was Esther.

Esther had deep brown eyes and a striking two-tone coat of espresso and cream. Margaret wrote the owners a check for two thousand dollars and led Esther into the back of her SUV. She said "kush" and Esther sat down.

Halfway home they hit the Dairy Queen drive-through. The malt was for Margaret and the fries were for Esther.

It only took two years for Margaret and Esther to establish themselves as top breeders. The buyers were other breeders or rich folks with big spreads on the outskirts of Houston or Dallas who amused themselves by sprinkling their pastures with eye-catching exotic species.

Margaret got so good at divining successful crosses she became known as Margaret Lady of the Llamas.

But there would have been no miracle without George.

George, with his measly one-point-one acre just inside the town limits, had been skipped over by the original oil boom, but was now getting some potential action from the frackers. Problem was, they wanted to set up operations right there at his back door.

George was a gentle soul who, as a result of his friendship with Margaret, had been taking in llamas that were not perfect breeders, or in some cases, just too dear to sell. Even though Margaret had several hundred acres and George only had one, he happily used his measly single acre as a run for Margaret's special rejects. Most became his beloved pets. A young llama named Cowboy was his all-out favorite. Cowboy was a direct descendant of Esther and had the same beautiful eyes and two-toned coat. His disposition, though, left room for improvement. He ate trees and picked on the mailman, and Margaret did not want to breed Cowboy's meddlesome traits into her herd.

At the time of the miracle, we were beginning our fourth year of a hard drought that had caused the biggest selloff of beef cattle and farm animals in the entire history of Texas. George's acre was stripped bare and the price of hay was through the roof. The only solution was for George to sell some llamas to buy hay for the rest.

By the end of another dry summer, George was down to a single remaining llama: Cowboy.

The price of feed rose higher and George did not know what to do. Margaret had wisely sold off all her stock right before the bottom fell out. Cattlemen couldn't afford hay anymore either, and were selling their prime breeding stock to butchers.

George began to wonder if he'd have to put Cowboy up for adoption. There had to be at least one rich Texan out there who would be unable to resist the young llama's striking beauty.

On the other hand, Cowboy was two years old and getting so rambunctious he would have to be castrated before any stranger would be able handle him, and George had put it off so long, he worried it might not change Cowboy's wayward habits anyway.

Cowboy had turned into a lose-lose llama.

Which made George love him all the more.

Having been left by his wife of twenty years when she ran off with a handsome human cowboy ten years her junior, George already knew that we do not go through trouble in order to become heroes, or because we deserve it. George believed that the only true measure of a life well-lived was kindness, which was why he was still living with Virginia, his ex-wife's mother who had Alzheimer's. When his wife left him, George hadn't hesitated for a single minute. He moved Virginia into the spare bedroom of his trailer home, and she too formed a special bond with Cowboy.

In fact, Virginia was the only person besides George that Cowboy didn't threaten, and George believed this was because Cowboy knew she was losing her mind.

Could he really put Cowboy up for adoption?

Everyone could see how much George was suffering. He was like an impoverished mother about to give away her child so it would have a better life with someone else, and we did not know what was best either. We wanted what was best for George, and George wanted what was best for Cowboy.

Well, a young couple who had recently taken over the old Smith place heard of George's trouble and went to visit. They told George that the frackers had paid them some real good money, and all they had had to do was let the frackers set up operations in their dried-up old peach orchard, which was really just an oversized backyard similar to George's.

George started thinking about how good it would be to have enough money to buy hay for the rest of his life regardless of cost. He remembered how the Hancock family had had one of those old-school drilling rigs—the ones that look like a giant bird, pecking rhythmically and incessantly at the earth—right outside their back door for fifteen years and all they'd ever said about it was, "It looks and smells like money to us!"

But when George went down to the old Smith place, just to have a look-see, he got a bad feeling. The fracking setup wasn't anything like a giant pecking bird—it was a restless, noisy city, fuming and flaring and strung all over with enormous glaring lights that never went dark.

"It sure ain't the prettiest thing we've ever seen," said the young wife, and her husband added, right on cue, "But it looks and smells like money to us." Then they all three laughed and George thanked them for their time.

He went straight home and stood there at his own back door, imagining all the fracking equipment and racket, and all he could foresee was angry neighbors, exhaust darkening the sunset, and woe to all things not made by the hand of man.

He would have to put Cowboy up for adoption to a good home.

The whole time George stood around imagining that fracking unit in his backyard, Virginia paced the floor, running in and out the back door, and slamming it hard every time.

"What is it?" George asked in a quiet voice, but Virginia kept right on.

George figured she was absorbing his anxiety, so he took Virginia by the hand and told her everything would be alright.

Virginia stopped pacing and stared down at the floor.

George said, "Take your time."

Finally, Virginia asked George if he wanted some ice cream and George said yes.

When they finished their ice cream, George sat down in front of his computer and posted a picture of Cowboy on Craigslist. Virginia stood behind him, looking over his shoulder without saying anything, which was her way.

Three days passed without a reply to the ad, but George just couldn't stop checking the photograph every few hours. And every time he looked, he wondered if he should change his mind and cancel the ad.

Finally, right before sunset on the third day, the miracle gave its first sign. Cowboy's image wobbled a little on the computer screen, then spoke: *Our cup is filling up. If we do not change, chastisement will come upon us.*

Dumbfounded, George jumped up and high-tailed it over to Margaret's, charging in the back door without knocking.

Margaret was in her kitchen, cutting tomatoes.

"I have received a warning," George told her.

"Well don't just stand there," Margaret said, as George stood gaping, backlit by the sun and letting in mosquitos. "Tell me."

The truth was, Margaret found George a little tedious.

"Our cup is filling up," George said. "If we do not change, chastisement will come upon us." He came in the rest of the way and closed the screen door behind him. "Cowboy's photograph spoke a warning—on my computer."

Margaret narrowed her eyes but kept cutting her tomatoes. She'd heard that Alzheimer's caregivers sometimes developed symptoms of their own.

"Are you sure that's what happened?"

"Not entirely..."

"And why do you suppose an apparition would want to speak to you through a picture of a llama?"

"I don't know. To make us listen?"

"You're grasping at straws, George. Fact is, you've got two choices. Either let the frackers in or let Cowboy go."

Well, there are natural disasters and man-made disasters, and times when no one knows or cares about the difference. There are times when people's moods go sour because they have just had enough. George was not yet to that point. He was only trying to get out of a single predicament: how to feed Cowboy.

He did not want to think about the complex forces tearing at his community. Big Oil, Big Ag, Big Government, the rights of property owners and the needs of people and their animals.

Soon enough, though, some of the people in Prosper began speaking out against the couple that had done business with the frackers. They called them newcomers, said they didn't respect their land and were going to ruin the well water for miles around.

Others defended the couple and said they hoped the frackers would come to them too. Times were hard and people had to take what they could get.

"Well I don't know," the beekeeper said. "If somebody ruins my well water, that's just not fair."

The lady who ran the feed store said, "Hell, once you start telling people what they can and cannot do with their own damn property, you might as well move to Russia."

The debate took a turn for the nasty. Those who didn't approve of fracking were communist devil worshippers and draft dodgers, and those who did were tearing up God's creation and poisoning their souls in greedy pursuit of the unholy dollar.

Again, George sought the advice of Margaret, because even though he had decided against fracking, he knew that his looking into it was at least partly responsible for riling people up.

Margaret told George that everybody ought to shut up and keep their opinions to themselves. And that her greatest wish was for everyone to just leave her alone.

But the truth is, in a place like Prosper, it can be painful when people do not believe in the same things.

It wasn't long before we reached a pinnacle of discord, and it split us right down the middle into two opposing sides. One side said, "Fracking will help us save our land and our lives," and the other side said, "Y'all cain't tell shit from wild honey."

George hated it when people took sides. He had never believed in anything much besides kindness, and kindness was just more his way of being then a particular belief. To him, the prophecy of the llama, while clearly true, was a curse. He couldn't go against his neighbors. Nor could he be untrue to truth.

He worried himself into such a state that after four days Margaret took pity and called me at the *Prosper Herald*. She told me to cover the front page with Cowboy and his message.

Frankly, the idea of a prophecy coming through an ad on Craigslist struck me as ridiculous. Being a newspaper editor, I had read about the miracle in Garabandal, Spain, and their prophecy came from an angel, not a llama. But Margaret is my cousin, and persuasive, so I agreed.

To this day no one understands exactly how or why, but when the article came out, things started to change. All I can say is that if you ever saw that picture of Cowboy, you'd know straight away just how soft those dark eyes could make you feel. And right below his picture and his message, was my recounting of the miracle in Gabarandal. I wrote that an apparition had brought the same message to an innocent girl: *Our cup is filling up. If we do not change, chastisement will come upon us.* And when the community stopped their bad habits, they were healed.

True, I did say that Gabarandal was in Mexico instead of all the way over in Spain. But I know my readers. Mexico is damn close. And if the Mexicans could make it work, we could make it work.

People got the point. We were all in this thing together. We had to believe, and we had to act as one.

When the frackers left town it rained for a week, and we all came out to cheer and dance.

A month later, we began to notice that the price of hay was still going up and most of us were still poor. Even if it rained for forty days and forty nights, it was going to take years to recover from such a crushing drought.

That's when George got his second revelation.

A rich heiress had sent him an email because she'd seen the adoption ad for Cowboy on Craigslist. She could not resist his two-toned coat and luminous dark eyes. She had a 5,000 acre ranch full of exotic species and could afford to haul water in direct from the Amazon if necessary.

What better home could a llama have?

George knew what he had to do. He took a long, sad look at Cowboy's adoption photograph, and with tears in his eyes, started typing the acceptance message: "I am so grateful…"

But he never got any further than that, because the adoption photograph was starting to speak the second revelation: *Gaze long upon the web but weave not. Behold and cast thy net into the vast unknown.*

George dropped what he was doing and called Margaret.

"Casting thy net" made her think of computers so she

called her nephew in Austin, who was a techie. The nephew told her that Google was paying people to do surveys, to find out what's hot on the Internet. *Learn to Talk Like a Texan* and *Think Like a Squirrel*.

"The hell you say!" Margaret said. "But what does that have to do with Prosper?"

"Nothing," said the nephew, "except that Google is investing a few billion in the project. Meaning someone's going to get paid to do the surveys. Why shouldn't it be you?"

"We don't know how to do any of that stuff," Margaret said.

"Just give me one person with a computer," said the nephew, who had a grudge against Google. "I'll set up the rest."

Well, once Margaret explained to everybody in Prosper what this meant—basically that a person could get paid for playing around on a computer—we all got together and voted unanimously to try it.

Of course, no one wanted to sit in front of a computer all day, but we wouldn't have to, because Margaret's nephew taught George how to "electronically replicate" himself a thousand-fold. He set things up to where all George had to do was log in every morning and his computer would mimic the behavior of different people using different computers all day long.

We got some money and divided it up equally.

Now I know all this sounds too good to be true, but if that's not the point of a miracle, then what is?

Sure, there are still a few of us who do not accept these happenings as a true miracle because George's apparition only happened two times instead of four as it did in Garabandal, and some religious teachings say you must have at least three. But when you get right down to it, we are not a community that stands on formality. We are a community in need of miracles.

Then, just a few days ago, George came running into my office and said he'd found his mother-in-law, Virginia, sitting at his computer. She was logged into Craig's list and grinning at Cowboy's adoption picture, and when he looked over her shoulder, he saw that she was typing in a message of her own: "Thank you, it worked."

WIND CHIMES

I am sitting on a barstool in Any Crappy Bar, in Almost Anywhere, America. A man sits nearby, and in front of the man is a notebook on which he has written: *Are We Living or Dying? Talk to me.*

I will talk to this man, and things will happen.

But first: a few facts, which I provide without apology for their unpleasant nature. I do not care what you will think of me. I know what I'm doing, and why. And I want you to know too.

First fact: I was beaten on a public sidewalk and raped in a ditch. All passersby turned away. Disgusted.

Second fact: It's a system. Beaters and rapists can be anyone. Policemen, legislators, judges. When a judge beats his wife, how can she find justice? She will be told it was her fault. Told to keep quiet, to seek counseling. Get on with her life. There will be booze. Or pills. Obesity. She will find her best possible poison.

Third fact: For me it was different.

I cleaned myself up. Did my makeup, my hair. I walked down the street in a white cotton dress with a full skirt. Mid-calf. Sash at the waist. I held my head high.

A man came along on a bicycle and said: "Will you marry me?"

A woman came along on high heels and said: "That's a pretty dress. Do you color your hair?"

"Yes," I told her, even though I didn't.

It was all a disguise. Just like when, a few years later, I dyed my hair purple, became a punk, and started hanging out in crappy bars.

Now, sitting here in Any Crappy Bar in Almost Anywhere, America, the man with the notebook notices me.

Are We Living or Are We Dying? The notebook is still asking, so I answer. "Don't be silly. The answer is both."

The lighting in the bar is dim, weirdly red and blue, and the man is looking me over, trying to figure out if I am pretty. Trying to decide if I will be a positive or a negative in terms of his needs. He checks out my body, my clothes and my hair, which was by nature blond but is now purple. I tell him my name is Alice, because I read somewhere that too many novelists use this name for their loser women characters.

Then it's my turn. I give the man my once-over, mindful that the low lighting changes his appearance as much as it does mine. His cropped hair has a copper glint from the red lights and his jeans are snug over long legs. There are lines in his face, and a bulging belly. Not so bad, really, just down on his luck, same as anyone who drinks in a bar like this.

He asks about my hair color.

"I'm a punk," I say, and tell him I work the peep show down the street. Door number nine. "It's not the real me, just an off-the-wall punk thing to do."

We both laugh.

I can tell he is getting a rush from my mention of the peep show, and sure enough he moves one bar stool closer. He slides his notebook along, leaving it open, watching me look at the words again: *Are We Living or Dying?*

"I'm a writer," he says.

"What are you writing about?"

"Nothing," he says. "That's the problem."

He's hit a rough spot. Hasn't written a thing since last November when he contracted dengue fever on assignment in Cote d'Ivoire and his boss offered him a seaside cabin on a remote island to recover. His boss was a proven asshole, so he felt suspicious, but he needed something and had no other offers.

I make no comment, which he takes as an invitation to continue talking.

Sure enough, the remote island turned out to be little more than a windswept sandbar with a poorly stocked general store at one end and a few cabins and palm trees at the other. His cabin was small, on a single, pitifully elevated dune. From the smudged window near his bed, he could see the ramshackle deck of another cabin. It had a desolate look, and seemed to vibrate in the heat and wind.

He read and slept for two days and that was going well enough, but on the third day, a fat lady moved into the cabin next door. She stripped off her clothes and hung what seemed to be a hundred or more wind chimes from every other board on her deck. The wind blew incessantly and the fat lady danced to the frenzied chimes, nude and screaming.

He lay on his narrow cot, in his own hot cabin, itching with sand and sweat.

The fat lady was enormous. A disgusting freak with a belly flapping out of control.

Fortunately, he had his binoculars.

I sip my Southern Comfort, and say I'm moving to a booth in the back to smoke a joint. The writer follows. We share my joint and it makes us mellow.

I decide that the writer is predictable, but he is not a bad storyteller.

The fat woman had insomnia, he says, and she danced all night, every night. Soon, he was sick to death of watching her ugly dancing body. He traded in his binoculars for a sleep mask but it didn't help. The fat lady's chimes were in conspiracy with the wind and the wind could not be silenced.

All the writer could do was lie on his cot and weep.

Finally, though, he had an idea.

It had not been easy to get the idea because of how the fat lady had swelled him with pain and revulsion. But he pulled himself together and found some not-so-fresh donuts at the island store: two dozen, glazed chocolate and raspberry.

He splashed his armpits with water and changed his shirt.

Coming face to face with her for the first time was not as bad as he expected. He plonked down two bottles of cold beer and waited while she gave him the once-over with penetrating eyes.

He caught her scent, pungent but not unpleasant, and took it as a sign that she was thinking of sex. He wondered if he could talk her into giving him a blowjob.

"Whad'ya come here for?" she asked.

"Your wind chimes are making it impossible for me to sleep."

"Oh those… I listen to them…"

He opened the box of donuts and offered them.

"Can't eat that. I was in a hospital. Diabetes. Heart."

"I too have been ill," said the writer, "and I need to rest."

"Oh. I'll take a few of the wind chimes down… Tomorrow."

"I could help you right now."

"No, I'll get 'em myself."

Her eyes remained fixed on the donuts. Poison.

"Take them," he said, and the fat lady seemed to fall into a trance.

She took no notice when he stood up to leave, but as he began walking back to his cabin, he thought he heard her opening a beer.

That night, the wind and the chimes and the woman howled louder than ever.

The writer couldn't take it. He needed a break. He packed an overnight bag and hired a boat to take him to a nearby harbor. He met a tube top girl and walked with her along the beach. He wanted to have sex but all they did was hold hands.

When he returned to his cabin on the windswept dune, all was silent. The wind chimes were gone.

An overweight, middle-aged man wearing khaki shorts and a dingy T-shirt was sitting on the fat lady's deck, drinking beer. Her brother.

The brother saw the writer, and raised his can of beer in some kind of sloppy salute, or toast. "Diabetic coma," he said. "She was never much good at self-control."

I tell the writer he should have kept those donuts to himself.

He gives me a hangdog look. "But why? Why did she destroy herself like that? Surely she had other options."

I am thinking to myself: Options. It can be tricky having options.

I want to explain to the writer that the flapping stomach was a 200-pound sail, built to withstand a certain kind of weather. Weather that only certain sailors understand. But all I say is: "Her stomach was none of your business."

"Ok," he answers. "But what about the wind chimes?"

"What about them?" I say. If he cannot understand the stomach, he will not understand the wind chimes.

"Think about power," I say, still certain he won't follow my drift, and not caring either, because I'm a doer not a talker.

There's a reason I work at the peep show. Why else would I get inside a box with one Plexiglas wall and take off my clothes so men can masturbate? Let them watch me pick their money up off the floor and feel superior. Let them think I need it that bad.

I don't need their money, but I do need an opportunity.

I pick my mark and, when he leaves, I take my revenge.

A quick injection is easily accomplished when a man is groping you in semi-darkness and believes he's in control.

I keep it simple, and suitable. Sedate, strip, drag into a gutter.

The drug is potent, and my blade too sharp to feel until it's too late.

How do I pick my mark? You'd be surprised at how many men like to confess their crimes in down-and-out bars.

The writer is still talking, telling me about bad men in Nigeria who make sex slaves out of girls. "They capture them and rape them and beat them and make them sleep in cages. They make them cook and do their laundry."

He finishes his ouzo, clunks his glass down on the table and tries to look into my face. "Someone needs to stop it."

I keep my face closed, tap the tabletop with a single glittering fingernail and say, "It's time for my shift."

I slide out of the booth and stand at the bar to pay my tab.

I feel his eyes on my back. Good.

Show World is only four blocks away and as I walk down the coldly lit street, I am sure I will see him at Door Nine.

THE GOLDEN RING OF NUREMBERG

In the central city of Nuremberg, there stands a castle with a heavy iron gate. Woven into the bars of this gate is a solid gold ring. Everyone knows the story of the golden ring. It is a story so old that its words curl forward off the page and hang like a veil over the eyes of all who read them. The story tells of a rich and powerful man, owner of the castle, and his daughter, the most beautiful young woman in all of Moravia.

In the spring of her eighteenth year, a remarkable young traveler strolled into the daughter's garden and captured her heart. He was exceedingly handsome, exceptionally clever, and had but few coins in his pocket.

According to the story, the young man knew that he could not hope to win the daughter's hand in marriage until he made his fortune, so he left straightaway to earn his wealth, but not without leaving a token of his good and honorable intention, serving also as indisputable proof of his ability and resourcefulness. It was the talk of the town, the seed of a legend—a heavy, shining ring of gold, woven as if by magic into the ornate twistings and turnings of the castle's iron wrought gate. Without a single seam, the ring was an incredible example of gold smithing that defied imagination and pleased the eye.

That is what the legend tells, but the legend tells a lie.

While the golden ring is indeed beautiful and beguiles the eyes of tourists from around the world to this day, what really happened was that the father flew into a rage when he discovered that his beautiful young daughter had fallen in love with a penniless rogue. He accosted the young man in her private garden, and challenged him to give proof of his worthiness as a match for the daughter of such an influential man as himself.

"If the look in your daughter's eyes is not enough to convince you," replied the young man, "I will create something for her amusement tonight while she sleeps."

The daughter went off to bed, but did not sleep. She turned, she tossed, she paced all night. At once beset with the happy anticipation of her lover's success and fearful dread of his failure, she seethed with curiosity about what such a clever and talented suitor might invent for her, and worried over her father's judgement of him.

At dawn the next morning, father and daughter collided in disgruntled surprise as they crept stealthily through the blooming lilies and around the fine green shrubbery, searching out the young traveler and his promised invention. The traveler was nowhere in sight, but in the garden they found his handiwork—a heavy ring of dull iron, woven into the garden gate as if by magic, without a single seam.

The young man had worked feverishly all night, creating his gift with the zeal and ingenuity that only true love can inspire. But in the instant that he finished it, he realized that he could not, in good conscience, marry the daughter. With exhaustion and the spare light of dawn came cold reason, showing him clearly that the parsimonious heart of the father would be sure to poison his destiny with greed and suspicion. Mourning the loss of his fair sweetheart, he understood the truth of her lamentable fate. She was her father's daughter.

So he left the iron ring as testimony to the momentous occasion of having fallen in love with a beautiful girl, and went to Spain to eat oranges and swim naked in the sea. There he met a dark-haired peasant woman who had pleasant, smiling features and who cared not a sniff for his fortune or lack thereof, nor for his talents, but married him because she liked his manner of laughing.

When the father heard the news that his daughter had been jilted for a lowly peasant who, if he suspected correctly, could not even claim to be a virgin, he went triumphantly to his daughter.

"Ha! You see, he was just an irresponsible, untrustworthy oaf after all."

The daughter, however great her shame in the eyes of her father, wept bitterly for the young man she loved. Such despair was not what the father had hoped for, and confronted with his daughter's tear-swollen eyes and ruined smile, he was moved to a generous attempt to fix things up for her.

He hired a crew of the country's best goldsmiths, and after a fortnight of working as if seven devils pursued them, the goldsmiths completed their work. It was a solid gold copy of the iron ring created by the penniless suitor, and it was woven into the main gate of the castle for all to see. The father paid the goldsmiths handsomely for their work as well as their discretion, then spread the story of how a clever young man had left the shining ring to encircle the heart of his daughter while seeking his fortune in the gold mines of Africa where, alas, he died in a cruel accident.

The daughter was filled with disdain for her father and left his home to live the life of a peasant. Because she was both beautiful and kind, she always had suitors, and many of these she took for lovers. Of some she grew quite fond, but none was ever known to make her smile.

THE MAGIC SHOES OF AMADEUS MOZART

There is a man in Ziguinchor who is surely the most dedicated shoe salesman in all of West Africa, perhaps even the world. I remember the day I saw him on Avenue Djignabo. It was a chance encounter, and destiny working the way it does, I was barefoot.

A heavy rainstorm had flooded the street and I was trying to cross it, experimenting with paths of least resistance. I hopped over, sidestepped and splashed through several puddles, then decided to skate across a wide patch of mud that led to the curb. Arms extended for balance, I had just started to glide and slide when someone took my elbow. "You're back!" he exclaimed, guiding me across. "How wonderful to see you!"

I stepped up out of the mud and onto the curb. I looked him over.

"You don't recognize me," he said, disappointed. "I met you last December. You were here with Babou, staying at Keba's house."

"I'm sorry," I said. "What is your name?"

"Amadeus Mozart."

Amadeus Mozart?

"Look," he said, putting his face close in front of mine, "I am the man with the shoes."

Of course. How could I forget the man with the shoes! Once, twice, even three times a day, he had come with a different pair of shoes for me to try. On the street and in the market he had found me, and once he knew I was staying with Keba, he was at my service there too. Never mind if I was sleeping, eating or getting dressed. I'd hear Keba laughing, then he or his wife would find me to announce, "Come. Your shoe man is here."

And so the shoe man became a part of my daily life. My Senegalese friends simply added him to the recipe of things that go on when you have an American staying at your house, and because they did, I did. There was, however, one problem: I didn't need or want any shoes.

I suppose you could call it a misunderstanding that started when Martin asked me to help him buy a pair of African sandals. Martin is a kind and mannerly American who loves to go shopping. But he could not drive a hard bargain if his mother's life depended on it. Anytime Martin went anywhere, the Senegalese street vendors licked their lips and pounced on him like wolves on a piece of fresh meat. "We can't let him go shopping alone," Babou had said, but after helping Martin buy gifts for his mother, brothers, sisters, cousins, aunts, uncles, friends, co-workers, and of course, each and every one of his seventh-grade students, Babou was not in the mood to go on a sandal hunt.

So Martin and I set out together for Chez Moro Market, and on the way we acquired several shopping assistants— lively young Senegalese men with a burning need to walk with us, talk to us, be seen with us, and above all, to help us spend our money. When we reached the market more people crowded around. I pointed at a pair of shoes. "Okay, Martin, those look pretty good, let's get this over with."

Everyone got excited. "You like? You buy. No problem." Hands began to pull, someone removed my tennis shoes while someone else tried to lead me into the shop next door where the shoes, he said, were much better. We soon had ten or twelve people talking to us in six languages. Wolof, Djiola, Peul, Mandigue, and French, with a few English phrases thrown in just to make us feel at home.

Martin tried on at least twenty pairs of sandals from I'm not sure how many shops. It was hard to figure out exactly who owned what, because one person or another kept bringing us shoes from all the other nearby shops. I was impressed with how it all became such a community effort. I tried on a few pairs of sandals too, just because it seemed to make everyone so happy. I explained to the salesmen that I never wear sandals because they give me blisters. They said, knowingly, that American feet have to get used to African shoes; that Americans and American things are soft whereas Africans and African things are tough, but that Americans can learn to be tough if they just keep trying.

At long last, Martin made the decision to buy, and he selected a pair of sandals that belonged to the shoe man I would one day know as Amadeus Mozart. I negotiated a good price—three thousand CFA, about six dollars—and we went home triumphant.

The shoe man did not seem disappointed that I hadn't bought anything. I guess he thought that time and persistence would eventually prevail in his favor. But unlike Martin, I don't like to shop, and I really didn't want a pair of sandals—two facts that did not matter one bit to the shoe man. He began to bring me shoes every day, and he was soon a definitive part of my life in Ziguinchor.

To say that Senegalese street vendors are persistent is to say that Michael Jordan plays basketball. They do not sit idly waiting for customers to stroll past; they patrol the streets, scanning for toubabs who, experience has taught them, have money to spend and little bargaining sense. They pull you into their shops and shove merchandise in your face, proposing ridiculously high prices, wanting to know if you are married, have kids, how long have you been in Senegal, what do you think about Bill Clinton, George Bush, would you like to go out dancing later—in short, wantonly mixing behaviors that Americans think of as separate: doing business, making friends, making enemies, making romance. The results can be amusing, even hilarious.

But then there are the times when someone says, "Please buy something from me today, because tomorrow is a religious feast, and my family is depending on me to buy and slaughter a goat."

My shoe man, though, he was different.

Undoubtedly, he was desperate to make a sale. But he never mentioned it, or did anything to overtly reveal it, except continue to bring me shoes.

We had a routine.

We would exchange the briefest of greetings, *"Bonjour, ça va? Ça va,"* and then he'd hand me a pair of shoes.

"They're very nice," I'd say, "but I don't want any shoes."

"Try them," he'd say.

"But, look, I already know I don't want them."

"Just try them," he'd say, and I would.

"No, you see, they are pinching my toes here," I'd say. "A little too small." Or too large, or whatever. He would examine the situation, sometimes making measurements with a piece of string.

"Ok, I'll be back."

And away he would go, diligent in his quest for the pair, the perfect, magic pair, of shoes that I would be sure to buy.

We never talked about anything but shoes when we saw each other, and even though we were together several times a day every day for weeks, we never became what I normally think of as friends. Ours was a special shoe relationship that left no room for the exchange of mundane personal information or private feelings.

We did not become friends, but we did become something.

Sometimes I respected his unflagging optimism, and felt grateful to him for not bombarding me with heavy-handed techniques like the others. Sometimes I resented him, stalking me at all hours of the day and night, his very presence posing questions that defeated me with their complexity and power. Are the rich morally obligated to take care of the poor? Was I rich? Was he poor?

I began to understand that the shoe man and I were prisoners of our own identities, unwilling performers in a ridiculous and misanthropic comedy. Everyone at Keba's was highly entertained by our antics, but humor is not always kind.

Why didn't I just go ahead and buy a pair of shoes, and put an end to the situation? I could have given them away, or burnt them in a ceremonial offering to the gods of cultural harmony and human compassion. On the other hand, the shoe man could have treated me like a fellow human being instead of a toubab with money to spend, and accepted the fact that I did not want to buy any of his shoes.

Either of us could have done this or that, but instead we remained locked in a finely balanced standoff.

Eventually, I left for Dakar—without buying any shoes.

Seven months later, I returned to Ziguinchor. I had seen old friends, made new friends, settled into a routine. I had conveniently forgotten the shoe man—until the morning he saw me sliding through the mud on Avenue Djignabo and finally told me his name.

"Is your name really Amadeus Mozart?" I asked him.

"Yes, of course. Is it possible that I never even told you my name? After all those shoes we tried on together?" He seemed to find it somewhat alarming.

"I remember you," I said. "But you look different now. Happier. Or something."

It seemed strange to be talking to him about anything other than shoes.

"How long have you been in town?" he asked me.

"About three weeks."

"Three weeks already! I have just returned to Ziguinchor myself a few hours ago," he said.

"Where were you?"

"In Guinea-Bissau. For three months. I was doing some business there."

The business must have gone well. His brightly printed African pants and a black Chicago Bulls t-shirt were new and casually stylish. I imagined him in pleasant scenes of success: quietly selling shoes in a nice little shop with a steady stream of friendly customers; confidently negotiating a wholesale deal with an international retailer.

It was nice to stand there in the street with him, chatting about normal things.

"You're looking well," I told him.

"Thank you," he said. "You are looking well too. But I see that you are walking barefoot in the mud."

Fat chance he wouldn't notice.

"As a matter of fact, Amadeus, I've given up wearing shoes in all this mud."

"That's not a very good idea," he said. "You might step on something."

"Well I'm doing it, and so far it's okay."

"Yes," he said, "that's you. You have to do things your own way."

"Yes. And you too."

"Where are you staying? At Keba's again?"

"No. I'm at the Hotel Mapala this time. Do you know it?"

"No," he said. "But don't worry. I'll find you."

That night, I dreamed that I was playing soccer, wearing the same beat-up pair of Nikes that I wore everywhere. Someone sent me a sweet pass, right in front of the goal. I ran onto it, kicking hard, but the ball stopped dead in the sand. Instead of the ball, it was my left shoe that flew up in the air and into the net. "That's not a goal!" the keeper shouted and everyone laughed. We searched for the shoe but could not find it.

I ran off the field, up the street, and into the first shop I saw. "Do you have any tennis shoes?" I puffed. "I need some fast, I'm right in the middle of a soccer game."

The proprietor, a dignified looking man of about fifty, asked me my size.

"Forty-one."

"Follow me please," the proprietor said, and walked straight through the rear wall of his tiny shop without even opening a door. I followed him through the wall and into a huge warehouse, something that could hold all the inventory of IBM, or maybe even General Motors. It was filled with tennis shoes.

"Do you want Nikes? Adidas? Converse? Perhaps you'd like to try a European brand?"

"Uh...Nikes would be okay."

The proprietor pulled down a pair and handed them to me. He said something in Wolof and his son arrived with a wet cloth. I cleaned my feet and tried on the shoes. They fit perfectly. "How much?" I asked.

"What will you pay?"

"Well, they fit exactly right, and I really do need them, but of course, things don't cost so much here like they do at home, so...how about, well, how about two thousand?"

"Two thousand it is," the proprietor said and held out his hand for payment.

"No wait! You're supposed to say something like twenty thousand, and then we negotiate. Two thousand! That's only four dollars! You can't sell me these shoes for only four dollars, that's crazy."

"Two thousand is what you offered and that will be sufficient," the proprietor said. "Now pay up and leave before you miss your game."

Then the dream jumped me back to Keba's house. The sun was shining, the flies were buzzing, and it was very hot. The proprietor's son arrived and said he had come to collect two thousand CFA. "What for?" I asked him.

"My father says you owe two thousand."

The proprietor must have decided that he did in fact charge me far too little for the shoes, and sent his son to see if I was still willing to make up the difference. I gladly gave the boy two thousand and he went his way.

The next day, he came again. "Two thousand," he said and held out his hand.

"Hey! I gave you two thousand yesterday."

"Two thousand," he repeated, so I gave him the money and away he went.

Next day, same thing. Next day, same thing again.

It was time to have a talk with the proprietor. I found him sitting in front of his shop, tranquil and handsome in an elegant blue boubou that matched the sky.

"What's going on?" I asked. "I've been giving money to your son every day and still he comes for more. Did you know?"

"Of course."

"Well how come you want me to keep paying for those shoes?"

"The shoes you selected are very special. You might even say they are magic."

"What's so magic about them?"

"The magic for me is that they cost two thousand per day," he said, smiling broadly. "The magic for you is... well...That is up to you."

I woke up early. The morning call to prayer was sounding, and the gauze of my dream floated away on its slightly haunting notes. I pulled the bed-sheet closer, listening, knowing that I would miss the sounds of daily life in Ziguinchor once I was home. What will it be like, going home? What will I hear, waking up in my own bed? It was hard to remember.

A knock sounded at my door. "Come on, get up," Babou called from the hallway. "Your shoe man is here." I heard him laughing.

"Tell him I'll be right down. And, hey, he has a name, in

case you want to know. It's Amadeus Mozart." I rolled out of bed and grabbed a pair of jeans.

"Amadou?" Babou said.

"No. Amadeus. You know, like the famous musician…"

"What?"

I pulled a t-shirt over my head.

"Babou. I'm coming."

I slipped on my tennis shoes without tying the laces. My comfortable old Nikes.

I stepped into the hallway and followed Babou down the stairs.

Amadeus was waiting, with a big pile of sandals. I sat down on his right and took off the Nikes. Babou sat down on his left. We all looked at my feet. They looked tired.

"They say you can always identify a victim by his feet," I said, "I saw it on a PBS special about crime-solving."

Babou chuckled. Amadeus continued to look at my feet, with an air of mounting sympathy.

I selected a pair of sandals with open toes. I put them on. Amadeus fastened the buckles.

"Did you ever hear the story of Cinderella?" I asked. "It's about a girl who lived a terrible life until she started wearing shoes made of glass."

Babou looked at Amadeus. They began a discussion in Wolof, ending it in laughter.

I hopped around the room in the open-toed sandals, trying to get their feel. They were light brown and woven from strips of hard leather. Stiff. I hopped in circles, around Babou, then Amadeus. I jumped up in the air and played like I was kicking a soccer ball.

Babou got up and played like he was stealing the ball from me. Then he pulled me back towards my chair. "Stop going crazy," he said.

I sat down and wiggled my toes.

"They get softer after you wear them awhile," Amadeus said. "You can wear them in the rain and the mud."

"You know what?" Babou said.

"What."

"They look nicer than your Nikes."

"They feel okay," I said. "I guess I'll get used to them."

"You mean you're going to buy them?" Amadeus said.

"I am."

"How much will you pay?"

"Oh that," I said. "That is up to you."

THE BREAK

James Boudreaux is standing in a hallway on the 55th floor of Global Fuels, waiting for the elevator to descend. It arrives, whisper-quiet, and its glinting metal doors open to reveal a wall of people, packed in from front to back. James looks at the people and the people look back, but blankly. No one moves aside or acknowledges his presence in any way. They are talking to their devices.

The elevator doors begin to close and James leaps in, forcefully, without a trace of manners or even the smallest gesture or glance that might help him feel human. He clenches his butt cheeks as the doors close pneumatically behind him. There is no room to turn around, to face forward with the others. Nothing to hold on to except other bodies that do not acknowledge him, so he locks his knees and stands stock-still, staring past the talking mouths as the elevator whispers its long message of descent. Down and down, through the industrial esophagus, positing each human passenger in its predetermined, requisite destination within the corporate body.

The electronic chip embedded in the topside of James' wrist has already informed the elevator that his vehicle is on the 25th floor of the parking hive, and instructed it to stop there.

When James backs out, no one looks at him or acknowledges his departure, except by reclaiming the space he had stood in.

Few employees have authority to enter the parking hive at two-thirty in the afternoon, but James has an approved appointment at MD Anderson. His wrist chip clicks him through security. He enters the hive, sees no one.

He removes his ear device, stuffs it in a pocket and grins, envisioning himself throwing it under the wheels of a truck once he reaches the highway.

The device begins to speak in his pocket: James Boudreaux, James Boudreaux...please restore your connection to the Home Office.

It is illegal to break the home connection, but James doesn't give a flying monkey's butt about that. A thrill runs through him, beginning in his gut and trilling up through his heart and into his head. He walks faster, stifling an ugly chuckle. It is not the first time he has removed his ear device, but it will be the last.

Reaching his truck, he gets in and roars toward the exit.

Traffic will be the problem it always is, and he is running late.

The vehicle James drives is a 1982 International Travelall, illegal on Houston roads except as an antique. He is not a collector but does not want to drive anything that could be connected to the master fleet. The fact that the Travelall is spacious enough for sleeping had once helped him feel self-sufficient; supported his fantasies of surviving outside the hive; but he's given up on all that now.

Stomping the accelerator, he tries to gun his way past a long line of cars waiting to enter the HOV lane. The engine knocks loudly and he downshifts, slips into a regular lane and slows to a creep. The sea of vehicles churns around him in every direction. It is not yet the hour of descent for the morning shift at Global Energy, so he is at least creeping forward. All three corporations—Global Energy, Global Drugs and Global Food—have distributed their work periods around the clock. If they didn't, no one would go anywhere.

James digs into his pocket, hangs his arm out the window and lets the ear device drop from his palm onto hot asphalt. Simple. Satisfying.

Traffic stops, inches forward, stops again, and his mind flies free to some upper stratosphere from where he looks down on the city of Houston. What he sees is an ugly, sprawling navel, feeding the controlling few.

Global Peace might have been nice, or Global Health. But that wasn't good for global profits.

The nurse practitioner, a burly man with hairy hands, takes James' blood pressure, temperature, and asks him how he is feeling. James clenches his jaw. The nurse knows why he is there. They are going to remove a cancerous growth from his chin. It is the size of a pencil eraser, hardly visible beneath the salt and pepper of his goatee, and capable of killing him if left to prosper. But they have to take his temperature first.

As soon as the surgeon enters, James asks her for three days off.

"One is the best I can do," she says. "They've been cracking down on us lately."

"Best kept non-secret in the country."

"What?" the doctor asks.

"The way everyone's dying of cancer."

"Yes," the surgeon agrees and begins prepping the area.

James asks her not to leave a bare strip down the middle of his goatee.

The doctor laughs, shaves right down the middle then wipes the area clean with an antiseptic solution that feels cold and unexpectedly slimy on James' chin. She raises a needle and performs a series of injections. The lower part of James' face begins to hum then thickens into something that is no longer part of him.

"Feel that?" No. "That?" No. "Ok. Good."

She starts cutting, her assistant leans in, and the smell of burning flesh begins to rise in James' nose.

"Sorry," the surgeon says as James struggles not to gag. "My assistant will be cauterizing blood vessels as I work. We can't have you bleeding uncontrollably."

Unsure of how long he can last without vomiting, James tries to imagine that he is strolling beneath a canopy of mature oaks instead of getting his face cut open in a cancer clinic. That's what his wife, Helen, used to do during chemo. Her visualizations went so far as to include a gently winding trail that led to a world of wellness, harmony and peace, but with so much stink in the room, James finds it trouble enough conjuring a single oak tree.

Thank God for anesthesia.

When the cutting and the burning are finally over, the surgeon puts her scalpel on a metal tray and stitches up the wound.

"You'll have a fairly long scar," she says. "About four inches. We've found it's better to make a longer, gradual incision rather than a short deep one. It reduces puckering, which is undesirable near the mouth."

James wants to say, "Yeah, and it would make me look as pissed off as I always am," but his face is so numb he can't make his lips do anything.

The doctor hands him a booklet with instructions on how to dress the wound and watch for signs of infection. "One day off is better than none, James. Try to enjoy it."

James grunts and leaves, hating, and pitying, the doctor. His own job is bad, but working as a doctor for Global Drugs has got to be the worst on Earth.

If James really tried, he could remember a time when people argued bitterly over whether corporations were taking over the government or the government taking over corporations. Now the distinction could no longer be made —did not exist. Or matter.

What remained of the country's health care system had become Global Drugs, and all of their operations were based on the twin principles of business and war.

Cancer was the top killer, and the War Against Cancer was still yielding the best profit margins ever not made public.

Once, considering such facts instantly set James aflame with anger.

Now, all he was thinking about was his day off.

Early the next morning, he drives east. The incision in his chin is throbbing but not badly. When at last he breaks free from the sooty grasp of Houston traffic, his hands relax on the steering wheel. He takes a breath. The heat and the parched, dead look of the landscape bear down on him, but the silvery line of pavement is now slipping neatly beneath the tires of the old International, eating up the miles.

Forcing down memories of nearby ruined rivers—the gentle Llano, the wild Pedernales, the mighty Colorado—James enters the nirvana-like state of mind that is the unique benediction of long Texas highways, and does not regain normal consciousness until he reaches his destination: Enchanted Rock.

The Rock is a formidable dome of pink granite, rising from the open plain, glinting through the haze of polluted air. For a time, it had lain beneath limestone and the Gulf of Mexico. During another time, Comanche and Tonkawa had watched its ghost fires, and listened to its night cries.

Helen, along with other dying women, had taken refuge there. They had been archeologists, spelunkers, and chemists. A few of them had been Texas Rangers. They had gathered at the Rock to seek wisdom and comfort. Banded together to learn, collect, extract, mix, and brew; believing in the possibility of medicine that could heal without destroying. Believing in themselves.

Now, there is only James, and the hazy air.

He stares at the rock and the rock stares back, elemental and wise.

He asks it to swallow him.

And waits.

WHEN THINGS GET TOO COMPLICATED...
AND YOU REALIZE IT'S TRUE THAT
EVERYTHING IS CONNECTED

Going through airport security they take my pocketknife, which I carry to avoid the use of plastic cutlery because we have too much waste, too much toxic stuff. I'm glad when they let me run back to check my knife but when I come back through security I lose track of my sunhat, which was tied to my cloth bag of organic snacks which they open and search because almond butter could be a bomb. Well, industrialized food and Big Ag are dangerous too, I want to say. Everyone is sick plus shitty health care, and who ends up paying for it all? We the public. But I keep quiet, they take my almond butter, I make my flight, and get home fine except no hat. Now I have to replace it because no more ozone, we have to wear hats.

So I call my brother and ask: Goodwill, REI, or online?

Not Goodwill, he says, and I know he's right because I'm not one of those people who can wear discarded stuff and have it work out. So I check online and find the hat, but ordering online means delivery vans spewing fumes, exploitation of warehouse workers, excessive packing materials, plus the cosmic unhealthiness that comes from anonymous transactions. REI has the hat, but REI means cheap offshore labor, diesel-spewing cargo ships, plus excessive packing materials. I could use my reusable shopping bag at REI, but I'd have to drive there; but my car is a hybrid, which is better than a delivery truck or a cargo ship, except I'd only be transporting one hat.

Hell, my brother says, you shouldn't have taken that flight in the first place, there's nothing worse for the atmosphere than airplanes.

Dammit, I say, everything is bad. You can't say one thing is worse than anything else and prove it. I'm trying to set priorities. Don't I get credit for all the time I've worked for free as an environmental activist? Don't I get to go somewhere once in a while? My flight was crowded, which reduces emissions, at least compared to private jets.

But we both know I fly crowded because I have to fly cheap, because of all the unpaid work, and thinking this makes me feel resentful about having to buy the small avocados in those plastic net bags which are a pox on the Earth. They start disintegrating into microplastics on my kitchen counter the second I cut them open, I can see the microparticles scatter, I'm probably breathing them, and I can't recycle the net bags anymore because China stopped taking our garbage. Yeah we fucked that up too, and anyway China wasn't recycling, they just dumped stuff where poor people live and left it there until it festered and floated down a river and into the ocean and strangled at least five majestic whales, a whole bunch of sea birds, and an entire pod of dolphins. Plus gave people cancer.

It makes me cry to think of it, which makes me think of people in Marin County buying those big, expensive avocados that don't come in plastic net bags. They can buy the best because they're rich, and because they're rich they also get all the green space, and they think they deserve it, but guess what, they are not the ones who worked to get that land into conservation, it was farmers joining with their former enemies the environmentalists, people who believed in something, who worked hard but never got paid, and now these rich people go around with superior attitudes, sneering at people across the Bay because they live next to a refinery, never once remembering that Larkspur was once an industrial waste site too. And they don't care that people worked their asses off for free, to protect that land they think of as their own.

It all just sucks, sucks incredibly, but then I realize that nothing is incredible anymore, and right in the middle of saying all this to my brother, he cuts me off because there's an emergency. *Evacuate!* he yells. Fire is rolling down the hill. The sea is flowing up the hill. Drop everything and run.

I'm not prepared, I say, no one is prepared, but my brother is yelling: *Get out! Now!* He never yells, so I run out my door and see that all my neighbors are running too. And I'm still trying to talk to my brother. *Where are you? Where are we supposed to go?* But he's not saying anything, and I get a really bad feeling, like something happened to him.

I love you, I say. I love you I love you. I want to thank him for being a good brother, always there to help me think. Please start talking.

Instead I hear him laugh, and I start laughing too, because now all the complications are being swept away, and burned away, and none of it matters anymore now.

ACKNOWLEDGEMENTS

During the tech boom, the San Francisco Bay Area was a place of change and movement and trying new things. A place where people switched jobs, interests and activities more fluidly than in other places. As a contract writer, I hopped jobs more than most, so how can it be possible that I am still enjoying the immense good fortune of working and sharing my life with a core group of people—people I laughed with and learned from, over the course of 40 years?

How many deadlines did we meet and survive? How many flavors and brands of software did we learn to digest? How many teams of "code slingers" used us as their translators? Designers of banking software and exploders of jet shatter canopies. Integrators of robots and factories of the future. Scientists racing to discover the human genome, inventing tools to analyze and annotate DNA sequences. This entire cast of characters needed writers and we writers were at their service. For a price.

Status-wise, tech writers seldom rose above the level of a necessary and tolerated servant, yet because our work was essential, and because we were good at it, we managed to extract a price for our services that most writers cannot, and that is how we earned our freedom. Freedom to keep writing our fiction, to travel, and join a workshop.

Our humor, our stamina and above all our respect for one another, made it possible to thrive as writers and human beings during an amazing, confounding and somewhat notorious chapter of world-changing history.

Jan, Judith, Layton, Craig: did we really do all that? I guess we did. Thanks for sticking with me.

MORE FROM JOHN'S MOTORCYCLE STORAGE AND RARE BOOK DISPOSAL

The following books from John's Motorcycle Storage and Rare Book Disposal publishing are available on Amazon.

WRITING FOR THE ABSENT READER

Author: Duke Miller, Aaron Asselstine and JT Twissel
Genre/Keywords: Short Stories, Magical Realism
Length: 244 pages
Release date: June 2017
ISBN: 978-0-9979426-9

These posts were taken directly from Tinhatsblog, for the most part, exactly as written. They are reactions to the events of the day, stream of consciousness meanderings, memories, love notes, and glimpses of works in progress.

LIVING AND DYING WITH DOGS, TURBO EDITION

Author: Duke Miller
Genre/Keywords: Magical Realism, relief work, refugees
Length: 323 pages
Release date: November 2017
ISBN: 978-0-9979426-1-3

A disjointed journey through a long list of wars and refugee catastrophes with everything you probably don't want to know about. Sex, drugs, drinking, gambling, death, dying, and destruction. Never carry a gun, always act innocent, and keep questions to a minimum because eventually you may not like the answers. Emergency refugee relief from the mud up. The big birds at Oxfam and the UN would not approve.

Made in the USA
Coppell, TX
26 January 2021